MELTING MOMENTS

MELTING
MOMENTS

Anna Goldsworthy

Black Inc.

Published by Black Inc.,
an imprint of Schwartz Books Pty Ltd
Level 1, 221 Drummond Street
Carlton VIC 3053, Australia
enquiries@blackincbooks.com
www.blackincbooks.com

9781863959988 (paperback)
9781743820858 (ebook)

 A catalogue record for this
book is available from the
National Library of Australia

Cover design by Sandy Cull, www.sandycull.com
Text design and typesetting by Akiko Chan
Author photograph by Nicholas Purcell
Cover image Ildiko Neer/Trevillion Images

For my mother,
in memory of Moggy

The train slows as it approaches the station, and he slides into view. He is not quite as she remembered. A little slacker around the jowls, perhaps, and not as bright of eye. Her heart pounds as she makes her way to the door.

'Ruby!'

It sounds like a cough. And now he is holding her, with no sign he plans ever to let go. She has waited a long time for this moment, and rehearsed it repeatedly in her head. It is an important moment to get right, for the sake of future retellings to grandchildren, if nothing else. The crowd eddies and swirls around them; she has this man clinging to her, as if she were life itself. After a good amount of time, and then some more, she pats him on the back, and he releases her.

'You told me to pack light, you see!'

Found accommodation, travel light, his telegram had read, and so she had filled a suitcase with sheets and tablecloths and clothes; a suitcase full of her new life, and his.

He laughs, heaving the suitcase towards the bus, and she steals a look at his body. It is leaner and more muscled than she left it. More sure, despite the uncertainty in his face.

And she remembers their wedding night, two years ago now, or near enough.

They had fumbled, knowing they were working to a deadline.

'Why won't it go in?' he had asked, finally.

She had been mortified. It seemed confirmation that she was, after all, abnormal. She couldn't manage this simple task that even her mother had succeeded at, for goodness sake.

She thought of the bull out at stud with the cows, the violence and conviction of its movements. 'I think you have to push.'

'Heavens!' He recoiled. 'Surely not!'

And so instead they had cleaved to each other all night, too aroused to sleep, too innocent to do anything about it. And the next day she had seen him off on the ship to New Guinea.

'Be sure to come back,' she had said. 'Unfinished business.'

She blushes now at her immodesty. But for weeks afterwards she had seen the keen, blind angle of his sex everywhere: in the railway crossings, in the bows of the violinists at the Palais. She didn't know how she would bear it.

'And how was your trip?' he asks, once they are seated on the bus.

'Everything was fine until Broken Hill,' she tells him. 'My godfather! The stationmaster called me in, and wanted to know why I was travelling at these times.'

Her voice sounds trivial before her husband, this officer in uniform.

'I said, "I'm going to see my family," and he asked where my family was. And I thought – well, I can't say I'm going to Brisbane, because that would be flouting the restrictions. So I had to tell a lie.'

She checks to see how he has registered this fact about his virtuous bride: he is listening intently, betraying no judgement.

'I said I was going to Redfern. It was the only place I could think of!'

'He must have thought you were turning tricks!'

His raucous laughter speaks of appetite – healthy, undamaged – and she joins in, reassured. She is sitting on this bus with a man she scarcely knows, a man with whom she plans to build a life. And perhaps they will be up to it, after all.

The apartment is modest, but he did so well to find it that she will not complain. He deposits her suitcase on the bedroom floor, and they stand awkwardly for a moment. She is not quite sure how to launch herself as a wife. There is a marriage to be consummated, but perhaps first she will make a cup of tea.

It is a relief to move into the kitchenette.

'How have the last two years been for you, dear?' he asks.

She laughs mirthlessly. 'Fine. Just fine.'

She had thought she would stay in Adelaide, but it had become difficult. Men seemed to be everywhere. Each morning, as she walked into the business college, there would be a flurry of hats removed, of conversations catching in her wake. She felt a little contemptuous – why weren't they off at the front? But she would still meet their eyes, just to see if they were looking.

And they mostly were, and she felt that jolting complicity: that men and women do things to one another in bedrooms. As if she needed to be reminded.

She went back to the farm, but even here things were not as simple as she remembered. Bobby confided that Father had been making the occasional error of judgement. Only last week she had found a stash of empty gin bottles in the barn, hidden behind a bale of hay.

'Mother seems a little miserable,' she says now. 'But I think she was glad of my help.'

Actually, there had been a strangeness between her and her mother this time. One evening, when she was sobbing on her bed, her mother had come in and taken a brush from the dressing table, and brushed out her hair in long, calming strokes, as she had done when she was a child.

Surprised by such tenderness, she was prompted to talk.

'I feel like Miss Havisham.'

Her mother paused. 'What did you say?'

'You know. Miss Havisham, the disappointed bride. *Great Expectations*. You have the book in the parlour.'

'I do not have any such book. And I do not know what you are talking about.'

Her mother had put the brush down and left the room, and she had reminded herself not to look for sympathy there.

'Mother's been working hard with the fowls,' she tells her husband now. 'Perhaps they'll be able to sell that accursed farm if the war ever ends.'

'If it ever does.'

'And what about you, dear? How have the last two years been for you?'

She is not clear on why he was granted a medical discharge from active service. He never seemed the anxious sort – but she is not sure she really wants to know. She wants to preserve him as the go-ahead young man he was in Adelaide when they went out dancing at the Palais.

He takes a sip of tea. 'I don't know that I care to talk about that just now.'

They finish their tea, and sit for a while in silence. Then she stands, and moves to the bedroom to make up the bed.

Somehow he has a better idea, this time, of what needs to be done. She doesn't ask why. He is attentive, even industrious, and she is relieved that they have been able to do this thing. That they have earned their status as man and wife. Afterwards he looks at her with such tenderness that she feels a surge of pity, and supposes it must be love.

'My Ruby. My gemstone.'

He curls into her, and his breathing slows into sleep. And so she is finally a woman, with her sleeping husband in her arms.

But she finds herself weeping, on this, her first proper night as a wife. She weeps for the two of them, in a bed together in Murray Bridge, wide awake, before New Guinea. She wants to be there again, and for him to be butting up against her, confused and almost delirious with desire, and for the beginning of their married life not to feel so much like an ending.

PART ONE

1

When Ruby first moves up to town, she stays with the Miss Drakes on Prospect Road, on the recommendation of Aunt Marjorie. The Miss Drakes have a horror of draughts, of catching a chill on the kidneys, but the atmosphere in the parlour – with the curtains drawn to protect the furniture – is the closest of all. Occasionally a ray of light steals through the gap, illuminating the cat dander that glitters and somersaults in the air like plankton.

'I've been warning you off tomatoes for years, haven't I, Ethel?' says the elder Miss Drake, over afternoon tea.

'Tomatoes never used to repeat on me, but now they do,' laments Aunt Marjorie, who is a fellow office-bearer at the Temperance Union and a frequent visitor to the home. 'It's a crying shame, really, because I did used to enjoy a tomato chopped up on my toast in the morning, but those days are well behind me now.'

Miss Drake takes a final, conclusive slurp of tea. 'At our age, we have found that regardless of how thoroughly you chew, *tomatoes will repeat.*'

Ruby is not sure how old the Miss Drakes are, but estimates

they must be at least forty. On the mantelpiece, amidst the doilies and trinkets, stands a framed photograph of a young man in uniform, posing before a *trompe l'oeil* garden. His legs are bound up to his knees in puttees; the strap of his slouch hat is tight across his chin. He is clasping his arms behind him, so that his belly juts out like a petulant toddler's, but he is a fine-looking man and Ruby's eye is often drawn to him. She has never asked which of the Miss Drakes he belonged to.

'We've found mutton to be a more reliable offering,' ventures the younger Miss Drake.

'You can't go wrong with mutton,' agrees her sister. 'I'm sure Ruby can attest to that.'

In fact, of all the challenges of boarding with the Miss Drakes, mutton is the most redoubtable. Not only the eating of it – although this does require a concerted act of will – but especially the smell. When Ruby first moved in, she would often wake gasping in the night as though drowning in mutton stew. To think she had once been vexed by Mother's mania for fresh air!

It is a smell that seems to cling to her, following her on the tramcar to work, so that she now takes a constitutional during her lunch break, rather than risk squeezing into the kitchen with the other girls. Only last week, Isla from the typing pool had whispered something about *mutton dressed up as lamb* and Ruby had jumped out of her skin – before realising it was a reference to Mrs Wright's ill-judged attempt at the Mainbocher silhouette.

'Above all, one must take proper time over one's meals,'

offers the elder Miss Drake. 'The world's gone mad. Everybody in a hurry, running hither and yon. No one with the time or care to chew properly.'

The eyes of all three women alight upon Ruby.

'How are you getting along with that night school? Not overdoing it, are you, dear?'

'I'm getting along well enough, thank you, Aunt Marjorie.'

'She certainly keeps herself occupied, practising her shorthand and what have you.'

'Well, I paid good money for that course, and I'm determined to make the most of it.'

Aunt Marjorie winks at the Miss Drakes. 'No doubt keeping busy with those typewriting machines and whatnot.' As if she knows anything about it.

On Tuesday and Friday evenings, Ruby catches the trolley bus along Grenfell Street after work, gratefully clasping a ham sandwich in a paper bag. As she takes the lift to Beasley's Business College, she feels she is ascending to her future. Everything at Beasley's speaks of modernity: the efficiency of shorthand; the percussive pleasure of typing; the mechanical sweep and shudder of the return key, clearing away the past and making space for the new. And then there is Miss Starr herself, formidable yet chic, emphatically not the sort to dwell upon her own digestion.

A quiet and orderly office is an effective one.

In typewriting, as in life, speed follows mastery.

Ruby transcribes these pithy remarks in shorthand, and then carefully types them out until they have become her own. Afterwards, she catches the tramcar back down to Prospect

Road and lets herself into the house. The blackout curtains are drawn, but she always switches off her torch before creeping into the bedroom, where the younger Miss Drake is already snoring. If she wakes up she will likely ask Ruby to help settle her over the chamber-pot, and some nights this seems more than she can bear.

On her very first evening of night school, Mr Singer had kept her late at the National Mutual even though she had expressly told him she needed to leave punctually at five. So that by the time she arrived at the college, the class had already begun.

'Lateness is the first sign of disorganisation,' Miss Starr observed.

A dark-eyed girl in the back row shifted over to make room for her. 'My name's Florence,' she whispered. 'Florence Lloyd.'

It would have been rude not to reply. 'Ruby Whiting. How do you do.'

'No businessman seeks a chatterbox as a secretary,' said Miss Starr pointedly.

Ruby had started the course with no intention of making friends, but soon Florence Lloyd is saving her a seat every week, and Ruby finds she enjoys her company. The girl is no beauty, and yet she has a boyfriend whom she talks about constantly, always referring to him as *Dale Robinson* – never just Dale – as if he were a matinée idol. Sometimes, as Ruby sits in the parlour on Prospect Road of a Sunday afternoon, discussing tomatoes and their propensity to repeat, she imagines the Hollywood weekends of Florence and the glamorous Dale Robinson: tennis parties, cocktails, jazz bands at the Palais. A wonderful life, surely, and on the whole she is glad someone is living it.

Florence often asks Ruby to join her for a milkshake after class, but there is always a reason not to – some darning that can no longer be put off, or a letter overdue to Mother – until one evening in October, when she has no ready excuse. As they walk towards Rundle Street and into the milk bar, she marvels at the way Florence is able to absorb it all – the office workers hurtling past with their briefcases, the sullen girl taking their order, the soldier kissing his sweetheart in the next booth – with no interruption to her conversational flow.

Dale Robinson has a dear friend Ralphy Phillips who already has a girlfriend which really is a crying shame because none of our set is the least bit keen on her and Dale Robinson and I both agree that you and Ralphy Phillips would simply be perfect for each other.

Ruby sucks the cool liquid through the paper straw, which becomes soggy in her mouth, wondering what Dale Robinson could possibly know about her. And yet it is not unpleasant to be so discussed. Absent-mindedly, she catches the eye of a man striding past the window; he winks and tips his hat, and she feels a surge of joy. Here she is, Ruby Whiting from the farm, sitting in a milk bar with a new friend, in a town that finally seems to be making room for her.

'You do get us a lot of attention,' Florence observes. 'You should be one of those model girls.'

'For goodness sake,' Ruby demurs. 'There are much lovelier girls out there.'

'I don't know about that. And I have news. Dale Robinson is having a twenty-first birthday party at the Palais on Saturday.'

'How gorgeous.'

'And I want you to join us.'

'Heavens.'

There are countless reasons why she cannot. She has promised Mother she will return to the farm at the weekend to help with the fowls. And she has nothing to wear: only her debutante dress, which she now realises – much as she loved it at the time – betrays her as country bumpkin. Most pertinently, there is no swain, nor any prospect of there being one.

'I still think you'd be perfect for Ralphy Phillips,' laments Florence. 'I just wish he hadn't been snapped up by that Mavis Adams.'

'Did you say Mavis Adams? If that's who I think it is, her father was at school with my Uncle Frederick.'

'That's Adelaide for you,' says Florence knowingly. 'Just a big country town.'

A double-decker trolley bus thunders past, laden with office girls and men in suits, as if to prove that Adelaide is anything but.

'Dale Robinson has another friend who wants to come to the dance, and you could certainly do a lot worse. We both think you should go with him.' Florence leans towards Ruby, grasping her arm. 'Do say yes, Ruby! I have it all arranged!'

There is something about the evening – the warm air spilling through the window with its bouquet of asphalt and gasoline;

the voluptuous milkshake in her mouth; the silences and sudden laughter of the lovers in the adjacent booth – that inclines her towards recklessness. Back at home, she takes her debutante dress out of the wardrobe and hangs it in the sunroom to air.

On Saturday evening, Florence and Dale Robinson come to Prospect Road with a man called Eddie Pickworth. It is immediately clear – both to Ruby and the Miss Drakes – that Eddie Pickworth will not do at all, but when she arrives at the Palais she sees a young man sitting across the table, with a serious, broad forehead and a steady gaze. After she has danced with Eddie Pickworth, and chatted to Mavis Adams, and then done her duty several more times with Eddie Pickworth, the young man approaches her, introducing himself as Arthur Jenkins. He has a delicate, pencil-thin moustache, and during the foxtrot, moisture collects there like dew. She feels an unfathomable urge to wipe it dry. When the band plays 'Embraceable You', his grip becomes tighter. He doesn't seem to mind the smell of mutton at all.

A week after the party at the Palais, Arthur still hasn't called.

'I'll ring him myself and tell him he has to take you to the John Martin's Ball,' Florence declares, which of course is terribly forward, but the waiting has become intolerable. *Arthur Jenkins*. The name doesn't trip off the tongue like *Dale Robinson*, and yet the following weekend, when Arthur arrives in his Essex sedan, it is clear – even to the Drake sisters – that he is a very promising catch indeed. After the dance, he drives straight past the house on Prospect Road and out to the British Tube Mills to show her his office. As soon as he switches off the engine, her heart starts pounding: could this be the moment of her very first kiss? But instead he explains, with great care, the intricacies of book-keeping during a world war.

'Naturally, good record-keeping is an integral part of accountancy at the best of times. But as you can no doubt imagine, international conflict raises the stakes still further.'

She feels enlarged by such remarks, and flattered to have been invited into his masculine world – but at the same time it is a relief, on the way home, that the conversation turns to hobbies. Arthur explains that he does not have a great deal of time for them, on account of his book-keeping responsibilities, but that he has an abiding interest in the study of German. When Ruby replies that she has always enjoyed gardening, he says something truly extraordinary.

'That's a turn-up for the books! We'll be sure to have a lovely garden in our future home.'

And at that very moment the car sputters and glides to a halt.

'Blasted rationing,' he says, leaving Ruby his coat as he sets out in search of petrol.

Outside, the world is entirely black, with scant evidence of the human. By the time Arthur returns she is shaking uncontrollably. She doesn't know if she shakes from the cold, or from his casual mention of their future home.

*

Early the following year, Ruby is joined by her sister, Daisy, and they move into a boarding house in North Adelaide. It is a great pleasure having Daisy with her, on account of both her company and her meticulous housekeeping. The weekend Daisy arrives, Ruby takes her out on the tram for a tour of Adelaide landmarks: the Fruit and Produce Exchange; the Royal Exhibition Building; the Botanic Gardens. When Ruby points out the Palais, Daisy gasps in wonder – *Oh, how I would so love to go!* – but Ruby proffers no invitation. Her own foothold within this smart city set still feels tenuous; a wide-eyed sister from the country would surely be a liability. But on the way home, she buys Daisy a snowball from Beehive Corner, for the sheer pleasure of watching her devour it.

Their landlady at the boarding house is a divorcée, a fact Ruby warns Daisy not to relate to Mother; nor is she to mention the frequent visits of a Dr Fitzgerald, with whom their landlady appears to enjoy some sort of understanding. Instead, the girls report that their landlady runs a very tight ship, and that the meals are nutritious and varied. Ruby now has a busy social calendar, but it is always a pleasure to return to the boarding house to find Daisy sitting in the parlour, working at some embroidery, or old Mr Wilson propped up in the sunroom, listening to the war report. And then of course there is Mr Steele, Arthur's boss, who occupies the large room at the front. *That's Adelaide*, Arthur had said when he first made the connection; Ruby had agreed that it was just a big country town.

Mr Steele keeps such odd hours that the two of them rarely cross paths, but the house feels different when he is there, punctuated by his confident step in the hallway, or his explosive laugh in the drawing room. Usually he takes his time returning home from work, stopping off in town somewhere for a drink and no doubt meeting up with a certain type of woman. One evening, Ruby sees him waiting out the front of National Mutual; for a moment she panics he is there for her. When Isla emerges from the typing pool, and casually threads her arm through his, she mostly feels relief. The following morning, Isla brings her new silk stockings into work, stroking them in front of the other girls as if they are some sort of pet. No doubt they are supposed to feel envious, but instead Ruby feels a triumphant contempt. Nevertheless, she always makes a particular effort to freshen up on Monday and Thursday evenings, when she knows Mr Steele will be at home for dinner.

It is on one such Thursday evening in September that everything comes to a head. Apart from the distant drone of the war report, the boarding house is unusually quiet, and Ruby takes her time getting ready for a night at the Palais. She has overdone it lately with the mauve, so Daisy helped her renovate her debutante dress: a racier cut to the décolletage; a yard of material shorn from the skirt. All traces of the 1930s removed, and of her old country self. *You look like Katherine Hepburn,* Daisy had enthused when she first tried it on. At the time, Ruby had shushed her, but now, as she applies her lipstick, she fancies her sister may have been right.

There is a loud knock on her bedroom door. Of course it is Arthur: he is always over-punctual. She lingers a moment longer, blotting her lipstick, but the second knock is even louder.

'Hold your horses,' she mutters, but even before she opens the door she feels a warning thud from her heart, as if her body knows first.

And there he is, holding a frangipani from the side garden.

'Good afternoon, Mr Steele.' Technically it is evening, but afternoon sounds more proper.

He bows, presenting her with the garnish. 'For the charming Mademoiselle Whiting.'

'Why, thank you. You're too kind.'

She remembers carrying on like this with her father sometimes, at the farm. Nothing that would trouble Arthur, if he knew.

But then he moves in closer, pinning the frangipani to her dress, so that she can smell the alcohol on his breath, and something else beneath.

He steps back and appraises her. 'A fetching picture. Aren't you going to invite me in?'

'Perhaps we could join Mr Wilson in the sunroom instead,' she suggests. 'I could make you a cup of tea.' She reproaches herself immediately for sounding old-maidish: why in God's name didn't she suggest a port?

'I think I'd rather come in here with you.' And he walks into her room and sits down on Daisy's bed, just like that.

Ruby busies herself at her dressing table, picking up her lipstick and compact and placing them in her evening bag.

He watches, amused. 'No sign of your sister this evening.'

'Daisy's gone home for the weekend. I mean, back to the farm. To help Mother. You know, with the spring cleaning and with one thing and another.'

She has warned Daisy, in the vaguest of terms, to be careful around Mr Steele. Though this was probably unnecessary: he has never shown much interest in Daisy, poor girl.

'No young ladies staying overnight either.'

'No.'

'None of Dr Fitzgerald's "patients".'

She would like to ask him who they are, these weepy young women who sometimes pass through overnight, the spare bed stripped so quickly the next morning they might never have been there. But to ask would put her at a disadvantage.

'A necessary service,' he says with a wink. 'But I'm sure you'd never put yourself in that position, Miss Whiting. Or would you?'

'No,' she says uncertainly – and then he settles back onto Daisy's bed and offers her a cigarette. In her own bedroom! The cheek of it!

'No, thank you,' she says, as if it were the only response she knew.

'Hope you don't object if I partake, all the same. It's been a long week at work. I'm sure your young paramour will vouch for that.'

'Yes, indeed. Arthur will be here shortly.' She takes her gloves out of the drawer and places them on the dressing table, as proof of her imminent departure.

'He's a very lucky man. And, I must say, a fine accountant.'

She had once suggested to Arthur that his boss had quite a reputation. That girls at work were implicated, though she didn't mention Isla by name. Arthur didn't seem to understand, or didn't want to understand, and she had felt gossipy and small-minded and left it at that.

'There are outside pressures, of course. Especially with the Japs coming into the picture. But I'm doing my best to protect his place on the reserved list.'

'Thank you.' The last thing she wants is Arthur going off to war. She likes having him around, for one thing. And it would hurry things up between them too much.

'As I said, he's a fine employee.' He studies her for a moment. 'And I'm sure you'd do your bit to keep him here.'

She glances at him. He is a nice man, really, despite his weakness. Surely he would not be making a threat.

He smiles. 'I've seen you in that gown before. But you've altered it.'

She blushes, despite herself. For all Arthur's qualities, he would never have noticed.

'It becomes you. You're a credit to womanhood at this time. Very resourceful.'

Somehow, Mr Steele has calculated her secret vanity. Not her looks: she doesn't feel that she owns them, particularly. They came on so quickly, like an attack of something. But her resourcefulness – this she has worked on.

'Though I suspect you could do with a few extra luxuries once in a while.'

She feels an odd sensation in her nipples. As if they have

been switched on, like light bulbs.

'Oh, I make do,' she says feebly.

And then there are voices in the hall, and a loud knock at the door. Of course it is Arthur: he is always over-punctual.

Arthur drives the length of O'Connell Street in silence, parking the car on North Terrace and staring glumly at the Palais.

'Turn off the headlights, dear,' she suggests.

There is a heady fragrance in the car that she struggles to identify; when she remembers, she hastily removes the frangipani from her dress. On the other side of the windscreen, eager couples make their way into the dance. The men look sober and adult in their dinner suits; the pale-clad women seem to flutter under the gas lamps. It all seems a little frivolous, when there is a war on and all.

Arthur clears his throat. 'That was inappropriate, that was. And I trust it will not happen again.'

'Arthur dearest,' she tries. 'Nothing happened.'

This is not entirely true. For one thing, Arthur came bursting into the room, flushed and handsome in his dinner suit, and bore down upon Mr Steele on the bed before the poor fellow even had a chance to stand. They shook hands vigorously, too vigorously, and volleyed each other's names back and forth.

Mr Jenkins. Mr Steele. Mr Jenkins. Mr Steele.

Then – and this is what feels irrevocable – Mr Steele stumbled as he tried to stand. And reddened, and righted himself.

'Well, I don't know what happened, but I trust it will not happen again.'

When he steps out of the car and comes to her door she can hardly bear to look at him. He is too beautiful, with his grave face framed by that white bow tie. Part of the problem tonight was that he had looked so splendid.

'Off dancing, are we?' Mr Steele had asked, once he had regained his footing.

'Yes, indeed,' Arthur had replied. 'Off to the Palais.'

And he had placed his hand on the small of her back and steered her out of the room before she even had a chance to say goodbye.

'Regardless of what happened, we will not speak of it again,' he says now, magnanimously, and takes her arm and guides her across the street. As soon as they push through the wide swing doors, they are engulfed by sound. Harry Smith is playing 'Cheek to Cheek' and everybody seems to be laughing, never mind the war.

'Look! Florence and Dale Robinson already have a table!'

She waves more vigorously than she might otherwise, and they make their way through the crowd.

'How are you, Florence darling?'

'Ruby, you are enchanting!'

'Haven't you two done well, finding a table like this!'

They are fine and ordinary words, of the type they have exchanged many times before. And a little later Arthur will lead her out to the dance floor, and they will dance well together, as they always have.

Perhaps nothing happened.

Except that, as Arthur guided her out of the bedroom, she had turned to collect her gloves from the dressing table and caught sight of Mr Steele's unguarded face in the mirror. This was the moment of intimacy, of transgression. There was a private resolution in his smile, exactly as she had feared.

2

It all happens so quickly. He has cycled over from the Keswick Barracks, and is waiting outside the boarding house when she returns home from work.

'Ruby. Let's go for a walk.'

She is keenly aware that her nose requires blotting, and she would have liked to have changed her blouse. But Arthur has a look about him that means business, so she threads her arm through his, and together they set off for the corner. The footpath radiates warmth like a hotplate; the agapanthus, shabby from the heat, crowds in upon them. She cannot remember ever having seen him so serious.

'To skip the preliminaries, I've been posted overseas.'

At the beginning of the year, when his exemption had been lifted, he had insisted it was because the Japanese had entered the war. As promised, they had never spoken of Mr Steele again, and yet Ruby couldn't help but feel somewhat responsible.

'I figure we might as well secure the war widow pension for you.'

'Is that so?'

At the corner, a cocker spaniel releases a cluster of expletives and she almost jumps out of her skin. *Put a cork in it, Winston,* a voice calls out. Words that stay with her. She feels not quite up to the circumstances, but time is running out.

He tries again. 'It doesn't do, you know. All those boys at the front, putting themselves on the line. Time for me to do my bit. And if I'm going to perish in action, you might at the very least get the pension.'

She has always liked him well enough, has always felt he was a go-ahead young fellow: dashing in his way, and of solid character. And he certainly cuts a fine figure in his uniform – if you overlook that doom-laden trudge, that self-pitying set to his mouth. Several times she tries to speak but no sound comes out. Cicadas screech relentlessly; the air smells of baked eucalyptus. Everything is pale and lilac and awfully far away. There is really nothing to do but continue putting one foot in front of the other, until they are back outside the boarding house, where he seizes her by the arm.

'To get to the point, Ruby, I'm shipping out on Monday. And I'm suggesting, with the greatest seriousness, that we marry before I leave.'

She would have preferred to have been wearing something other than her everyday office suit, wilting in the heat; and for there to be some sort of declaration involved; and for him to have been looking at her with an expression other than such wild dismay. But one is rarely able to script such things, and at any rate these were hardly the times for romance.

'Very well then.'

He sweeps her into his arms, and she is comforted by the density of his chest, by the friction of his chin against her forehead, prickly with the growth of a day. His smell is pungent but above all manly, and for a moment she wonders if she might weep. *My soldier fiancé.*

The following afternoon, Arthur takes Ruby to Henley Beach to meet his family. Mrs Jenkins is a sturdily built woman, with a bulbous nose and shrewd, darting eyes. She is full of news about a car she plans to buy – *Investing in a Studebaker is like putting money in a bank!* – which overshadows the young couple's announcement entirely. Mr Jenkins sits silently in his wooden grandfather chair, straight as a die; it is not quite clear whether he is awake. The place is like a Chinese laundry, with bed linen decked out everywhere: clearly Arthur's sister, Dolores, has been having some of her troubles.

To Ruby's surprise, Mrs Jenkins serves bought cake, which is dry and over-sweet, but presented almost as a delicacy. Dolores does not touch it, nibbling instead on her own sandwich: an elegant-looking affair with its crusts removed, rather like the cucumber sandwiches Mother used to prepare for afternoon teas.

But this is no cucumber sandwich. 'Mother's little helper,' Dolores explains. Her voice is soft and adenoidal, issuing from some fleshy part of her face. 'Bex and honey.'

'Keep your troubles to yourself,' Mrs Jenkins snaps. 'We're discussing the Champion model. By all accounts, it's a living room on wheels.'

In fact, Ruby is more interested in Dolores than the Studebaker. She has buck teeth and a narrow chin, so there is no real resemblance to Arthur, and yet there is something affecting about her gaze.

'You have beautiful eyes,' Dolores tells her. 'They glitter like diamonds.'

Mrs Jenkins doesn't like that one bit, but Arthur explodes into his delighted laugh. 'What did I tell you! She's a real gem, my fiancée. A ruby and a diamond rolled into one.'

On the weekend, the two families converge at the Church of England in Murray Bridge. There is no time to be a bride, so Ruby wears her best wool crepe, and a tilt hat accessorised with a sculpted ribbon. Arthur is a fine, upstanding groom in his uniform, and Mother the very picture of dignity and sobriety. She never intimates that she finds Mrs Jenkins common – it would be far too common – and yet already Ruby harbours a private shame about her new mother-in-law, who has sought to upstage her today in polka dots. Naturally, Father charms all present, with even Dolores taking a shine to him.

There is not much in the way of gifts, which is hardly surprising given the late notice, but Mother has the wherewithal to present them with the very latest edition of *The Green and Gold Cookery Book*, 'containing many good and proved recipes'. Folded into the back is an appendix of Mother's own tried and true recipes – her sago plum pudding, ginger cake and melting moments – transcribed in her immaculate copperplate.

'I will treasure it,' Ruby declares.

The ceremony is brief and to the point, followed by cucumber sandwiches in the church hall. Mother has baked a ginger cake, on account of it being Ruby's favourite; Mrs Jenkins picks at it with her fork, complaining that it tastes medicinal. After the refreshments, Aunt Marjorie sings 'Softly Awakes My Heart' – her formidable vibrato matched by her formidable cleavage, travelling down her chest in a tremulous line – with Mother accompanying her on the piano. Ruby hopes Mother might play one of Schubert's *Moments Musicaux*, but she is too shy to ask, and at any rate Mrs Jenkins has soon pushed her aside to thump out 'Roll Out the Barrel' – *Of course I play entirely by ear* – with her stumpy, dogmatic fingers. Arthur seems jolly enough, singing along and clasping Ruby's hand with a quiet, thrilling intensity.

Finally, after Father and Dolores have retired from the dance floor, and Mrs Jenkins has enlightened all present about the Studebaker Champion, it is time to leave. When the newlyweds arrive at the Murray Bridge Hotel, it is well past midnight, so that only a few hours remain before Arthur's departure. The room is not large, but it is tastefully appointed, with elegant French doors opening onto a small terrace. Arthur steps outside immediately for a cigarette.

Now what?

Should she change into her nightgown?

It is the most delicate item from her glory box: bias-cut and trimmed with ecru lace, with an intricate smocking she had laboured over for some weeks. On Tuesday, when it had become clear that marriage was imminent, she had tried it on before the mirror, and was reassured to find herself fetching. The unthinkable task was surely more manageable in the correct attire. And yet now it feels presumptuous to change without invitation. If only someone had provided guidance on such matters! If only Dr Wilkinson had offered more than those few stern words about *family planning*!

They have such little time; but even after she has changed and turned down the bed, Arthur shows no indication of coming inside. And so she is forced to take matters into her own hands.

Outside, the sky is crowded with stars, burning at full volume. Arthur continues to gaze upward as if he has not heard her approach.

'Just taking a final gander,' he explains. 'May be the last time I enjoy this view.'

It seems to her that he will have plenty of opportunities aboard the ship, but she holds her tongue.

'I reckon that must be Mars over there,' he offers. 'Planet of war.'

'Is that so?'

'With that red glow. Can't think what else it could be.' She has never known him to smoke so many cigarettes. 'Planet of desire, too. Or so they say.'

And yet still he does not turn to her.

Sometimes events occur as one might wish, but sometimes they do not. It is hardly improper to slip one's arm into the arm of one's new husband, but all the same she is glad there are no witnesses. The moment she touches him, he drops his cigarette and stamps it to the ground, and his mouth upon hers is a warm cauldron of spice and tobacco. Then he takes her by the hand and leads her inside, and she is relieved that they are back on course.

ravel light, Arthur's telegram had read, but of course she had needed to pack linens and clothes, not to mention key items from her glory box, so that now she struggles to heave her suitcase onto the train. *Allow me*, offers a voice behind her, and a gentleman in tweed takes her case and slips it on the luggage rack at the front of the carriage. He is tall and well built in a way she wishes she did not notice, but presumably too mature for active service. After she thanks him, he doffs his hat and follows her down the aisle, where he takes the opposite seat and disappears behind his newspaper. *INVASION: Allies Land in France.*

'Arthur Rightus,' groans a middle-aged woman, settling into the seat beside her.

Ruby blushes. Is the nature of her mission written all over her face?

'I beg your pardon?'

'It's the arthur-itis. Cold weather sets it off without fail.'

'I'm very sorry to hear that.'

The conductor blows his whistle, and Ruby braces herself for the thrust.

'Reading, eh?' observes the woman, once they are on their way. 'What's the book, then?'

'Oh, just a novel. *All Quiet on the Western Front.*'

The man glances up with interest. 'A fine read, that one.'

'What kind of novel?' the woman persists.

'It's about the Great War,' he informs her loftily, with the impeccable diction of a doctor, perhaps, or a professor.

'As if there weren't more than enough war already,' the woman harrumphs. 'Without folks *reading* about it on the train.'

Ruby returns to its pages, somewhat chastened. As it happens, the novel has some sentimental value. She and Arthur had spoken of it during their first foxtrot – they had both been reading it at the time, which she took as some kind of sign – and then over the months afterwards she had become so busy with stepping out with him, and then with the excitement of the enlistment and the wedding, that she never got around to finishing it. She had been reluctant to pick it up when he was off in New Guinea – lest it jinx him, somehow – but now that he has returned to Australia, it seems important that this small task is completed, before she gets to the rest of their unfinished business. Not that she feels any inclination to share this with her fellow passenger.

'What takes you to Broken Hill, then?' the woman demands.

Ruby is reluctant to admit that she is in fact travelling all the way to Brisbane, occupying seats that should rightly be reserved for troop movement. Although she is officially a married woman, she still feels there is something unseemly about her journey: she is heading across the country to climb into bed with a man who is, essentially, a stranger.

Over the twenty months of their separation, she has never for a second forgotten that she is married, but Arthur himself has come to seem less specific and more generic, so that his features are now less clear than, say, those of Bobby McInernay, who was unable to enlist on account of his childhood polio but who nonetheless cuts a striking figure helping Father out at the farm, and has a lovely smile to boot. For months, whenever she has tried to conjure up Arthur's face, all that has come to mind has been a hurried photograph from their wedding day, as if his head were forever half-tilted into the light, and his mother's proprietorial arm always around him. That aside, all she has had to go on is a handful of letters from New Guinea which, although full of facts and timings, contain very few clues about the man who penned them.

'I'm visiting family,' she tells the woman.

'Family in Broken Hill?'

'No, in Sydney.'

'What sort of family?'

'My aunt.'

This is not entirely a lie. Ruby has devised a circuitous route to Brisbane in order to avoid detection by the authorities, tracking from Murray Bridge to Adelaide to Broken Hill to Sydney, whence Aunt Marjorie, who has moved there to study nursing, will convey her to the flying boat.

'Your ma must have been sad to say goodbye.'

In fact, Mother had not seemed especially glad to have Ruby back at the farm – but nor, on the other hand, had she seemed glad to see her go. On the way to the station, it had appeared as if she might be weeping. *It's just the pollen, dear.* As the train pulled away, Ruby watched Mother's stoic face slide into oblivion, her cheeks shining with tears. But surely Mother could not have been crying for her.

'It's always hardest on the mothers,' muses the woman. 'Not that anyone gives two hoots about us.'

'Is that right.'

Ruby punctuates this with a full stop rather than a question mark, and picks up her book. After a disappointed silence, the woman takes out her knitting, and Ruby is soon carried along by the clack of her needles, syncopated with the clatter of the train. She places her book back down and dozes to a sense of purposeful binding – of things being knitted and fastened back together – and when she awakens, it is to a darkened sky. Her reflection has come into focus in the window; it is clear her victory rolls would have benefited from more lacquer.

Soon enough the train slows into Broken Hill. The woman packs up her knitting and limps off without a word of farewell, but the gentleman gallantly carries Ruby's suitcase onto the platform, even going so far as to suggest he might buy her a milkshake. Ruby politely declines, and all seems to be going smoothly until an orderly informs her she has been summoned by the stationmaster.

Shame.

She feels it physiologically; she can almost see it carved into the evening air. It is that childhood terror of getting in trouble, of being found out. But she reminds herself of what Arthur has been through, and steps into the stationmaster's office, resolving to be brave.

The stationmaster has a brazen handlebar moustache, and the slightly defensive air of a man who should be in active service.

'Final destination?' he barks.

'Sydney.'

'Purpose?'

'Visiting family.'

'Exact nature of familial connection?'

'Aunt.'

'Maternal or paternal side?'

'Paternal.' Why this should be of interest to the war effort is beyond her.

'Address whilst in Sydney?'

She is once again nine years old, summoned to the front of the country school to recite the twelve times tables she has not yet got around to memorising. For the life of her she cannot think of a single destination in Sydney.

'Where exactly is your paternal aunt domiciled?'

To her dismay, all that comes to mind is Fort Denison, though she cannot imagine this would aid her cause.

'I'm sorry, but' – he peers at her ticket – 'Mrs *Jenkins*, I cannot allow you to board a train to Sydney without a confirmed destination.'

'Redfern,' she says for no good reason, except that it has suddenly dropped into her head.

'Redfern?' He looks her up and down slowly, in a manner that can only be described as salacious, then dismisses her with a wave of his hand.

In Brisbane, Arthur has found accommodation in the guest rooms of an American widow, a Mrs Berenice Bower, who is mercifully visiting her daughter in Townsville the week Ruby arrives. On their second evening together in bed, he produces a book he has acquired from somewhere, and of which he has clearly made close study. At first Ruby surrenders to his embarrassed suggestions with incredulity, then with the beginnings of pleasure, and soon she feels well enough married, as if her life has finally caught up with her official status.

Aside from the ubiquitous presence of troops, Brisbane reminds her of a diluted, sunnier version of Adelaide, and she remembers that sense of promise upon moving up to town, when life still seemed ahead of her. She finds a job at the Department of Aircraft Production, readily making friends with the other girls, but every evening she detaches herself from their easy laughter, as a laughter that no longer belongs to her, and walks briskly back to the flat in order to prepare Arthur's tea. He is due at the barracks early each morning, so she awakens at first light to prepare him a hearty breakfast, consulting the invalid section of *The Green and Gold Cookery Book* – though, as she can attest, he is certainly no invalid. At the end of their first week together, she breaks out in spots. She is not sure whether these blemishes are the results of the tropical climate, or have something to do with her new wifely duties, and the surprising assertiveness of her body, but she reels from the bathroom mirror in horror, fearful of their impact on her husband. Fortunately, Arthur either does not notice or is too polite to acknowledge he has.

It is something of a disappointment that Mrs Berenice Bower returns from Townsville. She reveals herself as a woman of formidable opinions, with eyelashes so curly they look to be permed, and an unnerving, emphatic stare.

'If I had a nickel for every time Reverend Bower said there's no place like home,' she says.

'Your husband was clearly a man of sound principle,' Arthur observes.

'Sharp as a tack was the Reverend Bower. A pastor in the Baptist Church.'

'So you said,' Ruby replies sweetly. Already, the late Reverend Bower has been invoked so frequently that he has come to seem a fourth member of the household.

'And of course Reverend Bower, may he rest in peace, was a great fan of my roast dinner. The secret's in the gravy, you see.'

'Oh yes,' Ruby agrees. 'The secret's always in the gravy.'

Indeed, Mrs Berenice Bower's roast is a passable example of its kind, particularly for an American, though the lamb is not quite as caramelised as Mother's, and the beans strike Ruby as a little underdone: bright green rather than tenderly khaki, and not quite ready to relinquish their peas. The gravy is browned nicely, if somewhat under-salted. Unfortunately, it seems the potatoes have been cooked in too much water and allowed to gallop, and have consequently lost form; but the carrots are an utter credit to Mrs Berenice Bower.

'I have seldom had nicer,' Ruby compliments her.

'Just wait until you try my rabbit stew.'

It becomes clear that Ruby and Arthur are expected to dine with Mrs Berenice Bower every night, as she summarises her day's errands and good deeds. By her own account, she is particularly acclaimed for her *verve and vigour in the act of reading aloud*, offering this service several times to Arthur, who declines – graciously at first, but then with some vigour of his own.

'I'm more than happy to keep my own company in my reading, thank you all the same.'

'I think you'll find it's all about dramatic inflection, Mr Jenkins. The late Reverend Bower described it as the art of oratory and insisted I had a gift for it.'

Throughout Mrs Berenice Bower's soliloquies, Arthur nudges Ruby's leg, until she feels obliged to perform the necessary extractions, explaining that it has been a long day at the barracks for her husband, and that although they are grateful for Mrs Bower's hospitality, they really ought to be turning in for the night. It is always a vast relief for her to be back in their own quarters, and even more so to be back in bed, with Arthur's body beside her.

There had been times, when he was still in New Guinea, that Ruby had contemplated the possibility he might not come home. So many, after all, had not: Bobby McInernay's elder brother, Sammy; Mr Wilson's son from the boarding house;

even Eddie Pickworth, her very first date at the Palais, who had enlisted at the same time as Arthur. Such an outcome, of course, would be a tragedy for Arthur, but as he receded from her memory the more pertinent tragedy became her own. She imagined herself shut out from her future life, trapped at the farm with her parents, or in a spinsterish existence on Prospect Road, dusting a framed photograph of a soldier amidst the doilies.

But now that he is returned to her she has a clearer sense of what could have been lost. It is less her future as homemaker than this person in her bed. She maps his body with her hands and eyes: the boyish nape of his neck; the girth of his upper arms; those thick fingers that seem to carry a charge even when he is at rest. It can only be fate to have him back, so she doesn't press the issue of his release from active service; and at any rate, he is still making an honourable contribution through his book-keeping.

However, Mrs Berenice Bower cannot leave well enough alone – *Forgive my curiosity, Mr Jenkins, but a landlady is entitled to know, why exactly did they send you back from New Guinea?* – until Arthur's deflections become more perfunctory, and his urgent nudges more frequent. The last straw is when Mrs Berenice Bower enquires, over her acclaimed rabbit stew, whether Ruby is still *regular,* given the young couple's clear enthusiasm for – how can she put this – *repopulating Australia,* if you will forgive her for prying, but of course the walls are very thin and she is in no way squeamish about such issues, given some of the things she has seen whilst volunteering at the hospital.

What type of thing is this to say at the table, and before a returned serviceman at that?

Arthur turns to Ruby in mute despair; she summons up a brand-new matronly manner that brooks no argument, thanking Mrs Berenice Bower for her hospitality up to this point, but informing her that she and Arthur will be dining privately in their rooms from this day on. Thenceforth, Mrs Berenice Bower's gift for oratory is contained by the adjacent wall, and Ruby is glad to be back in charge of their meals.

As she cooks, Arthur parks himself at the table, reading through his pile of books from the local library, mostly on historic military campaigns – hardly the most restorative material, in her private opinion – or tuning into *Deutsch Kurz-wellensender* to practise his German, which strikes her as a risky activity indeed in such close quarters to Mrs Berenice Bower. Sometimes, as he *keeps his own company in his reading*, she glances over at him and is ambushed by something: a release of the salivary glands, an internal duress. She feels almost pained by his serene brow, his steady gaze. Of course he was other even before the war, as any man must be; but he has returned encased in a greater otherness.

In bed, she often senses that he too is awake, and yet there is some invisible boundary that she cannot traverse, something that stops her reaching for him and slinging a leg across his body. At first, she is alarmed by his nightmares, but she comes to welcome these disturbances as an excuse to turn to him, mooring her breath to his, her heartbeat to his, so that they plummet together back down the leagues of sleep, like that parachutist and his sweetheart she saw on a war report. When it is he who approaches her in the night, she receives him gratefully. He is initially too polite even to look at her breasts, so that she fears her naked form displeases him, but in time he becomes accustomed to taking them in his hands, and nuzzling them in a way she is not persuaded is proper – but whom could she possibly ask? – and at any rate she supposes one should do what one can for a returned serviceman, and besides she rather likes it. As he labours atop her, there are moments in which she meets his eye and briefly imagines she understands him, though at the cumulative instant his gaze always becomes opaque, and he retreats once more into his private world.

A month after Ruby's arrival, on the morning of Arthur's first proper rostered day off, she brings him breakfast in bed, the toast spread with the final remnants of Mother's apricot jam.

'Never mind the crumbs,' she says recklessly, as she kisses him goodbye.

'Leaving me at the scene of the crime, are you?'

She blushes, but all the way to work she cannot stop thinking about the previous evening, in which their exertions had resulted in an unprecedented level of mutual success, and as the bus rolls over the bumpy road, and the other passengers swing around her, she replays a key moment repeatedly in her mind – particularly the way Arthur actually held her gaze – to the extent that her body threatens to remember also, a little too effectively, and she hastily redirects her attention to the passing streets. Nonetheless, she arrives at work in a state of some agi-tation, so that when Mrs Ashley-Brown asks if she is feeling unwell she replies on a whim that she has a headache, and since it is a quiet day at the office she is soon back on the bus, flushed and craven, wondering what she will possibly say to her sleep-addled husband when he answers the door.

Fortunately it is a Wednesday, so Mrs Berenice Bower is offering her services to the cheer-up society, but Ruby hesitates at the front nonetheless, before rapping on the window.

He opens the door with that small furrow in his forehead.

'Are you quite all right, dear?' he asks.

'Quite all right.'

He grasps her hand – *In that case* – and leads her into the bedroom.

Later that afternoon, she wakes to find her husband looking at her. As she reaches over to smooth his brow, he utters words he has not uttered previously, either before or in the immediate aftermath of the wedding. She has never used such words either, but she reciprocates easily, as if such words only needed to be earned by a month together in bed, where they could be found to be true.

4

R uby has anticipated this moment since girlhood: the proper unpacking of her glory box, the setting of the stage for her adult life. She has found a little cottage on Cross Road – or *Cross Roads*, as the locals call it, even though it is only one road as far as the eye can see. Daisy brings up Mother's second-best silver tea service from the farm, polishing it until every surface is a mirror, and when Ruby arranges it on the sideboard it lifts the tone immeasurably. On Daisy's recommendation, she allocates a white tea towel for cutlery and a plaid one for saucepans, and irons the tablecloth directly onto the table, so that all is spick and span for Arthur's arrival.

And yet even once demobilisation is complete, and Arthur is restored to her bed, a feeling of home remains elusive. Every morning she sees him off to work, and is reassured by the purposeful traffic outside their gate, by the sense of everyone properly getting on with their business. But after he has driven off, she gazes along the span of Cross Roads from the Adelaide foothills all the way out to the west and feels the emptiness rush in at her, as if she were living on a road from nowhere to nowhere. As if the entire city were built on a desert, and her fledgling rose garden the thinnest of veneers. No doubt it would help if Arthur stopped bringing the newspapers into the house, with their reports from Belsen or Auschwitz or Nuremberg. Or if Florence ceased regaling her with those appalling stories from Dale Robinson. *You would never believe what they found when they returned to collect the wounded.* She is glad that Arthur, at least, has the discretion to keep such things to himself, and urges Florence to encourage Dale in a hobby.

When she sees a job advertised for a part-time telegraph operator at the General Post Office, she realises this is exactly what she needs: to be back in the thick of it, a moving part in the moving world. And so, after four months of training, she becomes an official operator of the Murray Multiplex machines, transmitting and receiving telegrams from every capital city in Australia. *Please wire money* STOP *Tell Ellie I love her* STOP *Will honour your decision either way* STOP *Still no official information available* STOP *A baby boy but that does not bring him back* STOP *God bless you both on your marriage* STOP

It must be the noisiest room in Adelaide, and she returns home energised from her shifts, impatient to get on with things: the housework, the lovemaking, the starting of a family. Unfortunately, Arthur's approach to their evenings is somewhat more stolid. It becomes clear that he expects her to sit alongside him as he reads, on the uncomfortable chaise longue in the front room – all very well for him since he gets the backrest – where he drapes an arm around her shoulders or rests a heavy hand on her leg, like a fleshy type of shackle. Nobody had warned her of this aspect of married life: a husband's constant need for physical contact. Now that she is out during the day, all of her wifely work needs to be crammed into the evening, but Arthur fails to appreciate that the successful completion of chores is more important than any amount of sitting and being touched. For a time, Ruby submits to being patted, all the while revising the list of things that need to be done: the oats to be soaked; the socks to be darned; the laundry to be brought in and folded. Then, in search of achievement, she tries knitting, but the clinking needles only exacerbate his tic. He can cope better with the quiet rhythms of needlepoint, but there is only so much needlepoint one wishes to do whilst the ironing is still pending. It is always a relief when he nods off beside her, and she can remove his hand from her leg and escape the chaise longue, liberated into her chores.

Apart from visits to see his family at Henley Beach, Arthur is reluctant to get out much at all, and would be quite happy for the two of them to spend their entire weekends on that chaise longue, meals excepted. Ruby fears that if she does not make an effort to get their social life going again they will become recluses, and phones Florence in a state of some desperation. As it happens, Florence is organising a table for the Semaphore Palais, to celebrate the anniversary of Victory in the Pacific, and would only be too delighted for Ruby and Arthur to join them.

Despite some grumbles, Arthur scrubs up admirably in his old suit, and as they drive out to Semaphore she is hopeful they might recover something of their former selves. And when they arrive, who should they see but Mavis Adams! She is as sturdy and handsome as Ruby remembers, and as endlessly interested in everything, and as endlessly certain about everything.

'Ruby, glorious creature! You haven't changed a bit. Allow me to introduce my husband, Captain Bill Clarkson from the RAAF.'

The last time Ruby and Mavis crossed paths, Mavis had been on the arm of Ralphy Phillips. It is clear immediately that Bill Clarkson is a superior catch. He has that pilot glamour about him, though not in the aloof manner you often saw. Instead, all parts of his body seem to be in motion, from his eyebrows to his hands, which are more expressive than might be desirable in a man.

He takes Ruby's hand in his own and kisses it.

'Rubies are red, violets are blue. Sweet Ruby Rose, may I dance with you?'

'The man's a rogue,' Mavis says. 'Don't trust a word he says.'

Ruby doesn't think she needs the warning. She knows the sort. As Bill guides her to the dance floor, she is reminded of Father: the attentiveness, the charm, the desperate need to be liked.

'Follow the nags, Ruby Rose?'

'From time to time.'

'Ever place a bet?'

She glances at Arthur, who seems safely ensconced in conversation with Dale Robinson.

'Don't mind a little flutter, once in a while.'

He laughs robustly. 'A woman after my own heart.'

It is a lark to dance with him, but he is not the sort you would choose to marry. There is something indiscriminate about the way he sprays around his charm, grinning at the other couples as they pass, winking at the men. Florence appears to be quite besotted, swirling up to them and almost intercepting – like a man! – so that Bill has no choice but to ask her for the next dance.

Ruby takes the foxtrot with Arthur, who may be less nimble on his feet but is more reliably present.

'I'm not entirely convinced by this Bill Clarkson fellow,' he mutters. 'Big-noting himself about land speed records, and this, that and the other.'

At supper, Bill orders a bottle of French champagne so that they can toast victory yet again.

'To Victory in the Pacific!'

'Can you imagine, a year already?' gasps Mavis.

'It's certainly hard to believe,' Ruby agrees.

On VP Day, she and Arthur had still been in Brisbane. Although he did not usually care for crowds, he had grabbed her by the hand and taken her to the streets. In Queen Street, just outside Custom House, a young woman had seized him by the shoulders and planted a kiss smack on his lips, before moving along to the next group of servicemen. Arthur could not stop laughing, surrounded by those honking horns, the confetti caught in his eyelashes and on his tongue.

'You must tell your Uncle Frederick that Samuel is retiring from the Law,' says Mavis. 'But that his eldest – that's Rupert, whom you may know through Florence – he married that lovely Blackburn girl, I mean the younger one. What was her name? It's on the tip of my tongue.'

The bubbles seem to have gone to Ruby's head, and she finds Mavis's conversation hard to follow. Instead, her attention keeps drifting towards the men.

'She's a beauty,' Bill says to Arthur. 'We're in with a chance at the new Sydney to Hobart, I reckon.'

'Never been one for sailing,' Arthur replies, as if he had even tried.

'Come out one weekend and give it a burl.'

'Don't know that I care to, thank you very much. Tennis does me nicely.'

'Anyway, Rupert has it all in hand,' Mavis reassures her. 'He's still a keen sportsman, of course. Joins Bill for the occasional round of golf. That's Samuel, I mean, not Rupert. Though Rupert's always had that unbeatable backhand.'

Ruby inadvertently catches Bill's eye, and soon enough she feels his hand on her lower back, guiding her to the dance floor. There is something purposeful about the way he steers her. The way he pilots her, perhaps. She realises she likes it.

'Say, what did you make of the Cup last year?' he asks.

'My father had a lot to say about that Rainbird. Reckons she robbed him of a fortune.'

He laughs. 'Your father wasn't the only one to be hoodwinked. Proud moment for South Australia all the same.'

Other couples sail by, silent and earnest, succumbing to Harry Smith's muted trumpet. Ruby might have liked to do the same, but Bill talks too much for the music properly to take hold.

He leans in closer.

'The last time we ventured out here we had quite a scene, let me tell you. Mavis was riding pillion, wearing a brand-new frock. Pretty as a picture, just as you'd expect. So there we are, going at a good clip, and all of a sudden I sense Mavis getting a little hot under the collar. Wasn't sure why, so I gave her hand a couple of tight squeezes. Our secret signal, you see. That all is well.'

Ruby feels curiously excluded from this signal; even robbed of something.

'And, God bless her, Mavis squeezed right back.'

Mavis passes by with Dale Robinson. 'Darling,' she calls out. 'I hope you're not telling tales out of school. I'd be frightfully embarrassed if you were.'

'Just relaying the story of our recent mishap.'

Mavis tinkles with a laughter that does not seem remotely embarrassed.

'It was only when we arrived at Semaphore that everything became clear. Blow me down, but hadn't her frock gone and got itself all tangled up in the back wheel!'

'Goodness.'

'The entire backside completely ripped off!' He hoots. 'Must have given our fellow motorists a fine show. Remarkable we weren't stopped for public indecency.'

The story has a curious effect on her, and she files it away for later. She can see the scene clearly: Bill steering the motorcycle down the highway with heedless cheer; his near-naked, unflappable wife riding pillion behind him. It is a vision that remains with her long after that evening, sometimes rising unbidden across the inside of her eyelids as she lies beneath Arthur in bed. At first, the mental picture is of Bill and Mavis, but in time Mavis transforms into a version of Ruby. She is in a state of reckless dishabille; air roars against the backs of her legs; her garter straps are visible for all to see. Bill sits ahead, gripping the handlebars, and together they grin against the wind, leaving scandal in their wake.

The following month, Arthur is posted to Melbourne, and they do not see Bill and Mavis again for some time, which is likely all for the best.

5

It seems to Ruby that Arthur has more of a spring in his step in Melbourne, possibly on account of being away from his mother. Certainly, he is more inclined to try new things. One night he returns home from work with a brand-new Canon, demonstrating the shutter speed – which she agrees is decidedly modern – and holding the lens up to the light. *Fast glass on this one. No doubt about it.*

To Ruby's surprise, he proves to have quite an eye. She herself is his favourite subject, and over the months of her confinement he becomes adept at concealing her bulge. Sometimes the photo shoots can be trying, as she is forced to hold a pose interminably while he experiments with lighting and camera angles, but she co-operates because it is clear that it calms him, and it can only be a good thing that he has a hobby. And occasionally an image might emerge from his darkroom that offers some truth about herself, or at least a version of herself in which she would like to believe.

But then the baby comes along, and either Arthur loses interest in Ruby as a subject or Ruby loses interest in herself, and before she knows it the camera has remained in its case for nearly a year. None of which troubles her at first, so entranced is she by little Eva. Even Glenda from next door, who is an expert on everything from Dr Spock to Ingrid Bergman, remarks that she *has never met so personable a baby.* It is only when the child is weaned, and has started sleeping through the night, that Ruby wonders whether she might have lost something of herself, and become a little stodgy and stale.

'Darling, you couldn't be stodgy and stale if you tried,' says Glenda. 'But I know how easy it is to let oneself go. After William came along, I did a modelling course and it brightened me up no end.'

'What sort of modelling course?'

'Oh, you know. Deportment and make-up application and so on. At the Bambi Shmith Modelling College in the city.'

'Not *the* Bambi Shmith? That lovely creature in the *Weekly*?'

'The very same. And very clever, I believe, on the violin. People used to go to the Symphony just to look at her.'

Ruby phones the East Melbourne offices that very morning. Although she blanches at the cost, it is immediately clear that she has to do it. That evening, she prepares a creamy sago pudding for dessert, which complements the stewed apples admirably. It is only after Arthur has asked for a second helping that she mentions the course, carefully spelling out the benefits for his art photography.

'A marvellous idea,' he agrees, and indeed he is inspired to take out his camera again that very night.

*

During their photo shoots, Arthur has always been fascinated by Ruby's disrobing. She submits, of course, but thinks of it as somewhat hackneyed – a children's game with a single outcome: *Peekaboo.* How much more interesting to put together an outfit; how much more erotic, even.

Today, she starts by pulling on her stockings and fastening the stays. Then she buttons up the silk blouse she has just mended. Never mind that it is a bit worn under the collar; she ties her scarf a little raffishly, as she saw in last month's *Vogue.* Next she steps into the skirt, which she has brought up to this season's length, and slips on the shoes, resoled and really as good as new. Finally, she pulls on her new cashmere gloves – her only indulgence – in the perfect fawn to complement the skirt. As she turns to the mirror and sucks in her cheeks, she dares to think it: she looks smart. And not just smart, but resourceful. It's all very well to have an expense account at David Jones, but some people have to make do with the materials on hand, and perhaps develop a keener, more exacting taste as a consequence.

Of course Granny Jenkins never waits to be invited to Melbourne: she just announces she is coming. And on this occasion in particular, Ruby wishes she was not there. But now that she is all put together, she feels better able to handle her mother-in-law, and so she scoops up the baby and knocks on Granny's bedroom door.

'Time to go!'

Naturally, the old woman takes her time, emerging in a mint-green twin set, accessorised with a maroon hat. Ruby is unsure whether this is a deliberate act of sabotage. Surely even

Granny Jenkins knows that *red and green should never be seen.*

'I do so like bright colours,' she says defiantly. 'None of those dreary hues you see today.' Her eyes alight upon Ruby's gloves. 'But I couldn't find my gloves anywhere. Eva must have taken them.'

'Bot-tle!' insists Eva.

'For goodness sake,' says Ruby. 'The baby hasn't been near your room.'

'Why don't you give me those beige ones?' Granny Jenkins suggests. 'You can wear your other pair. The salmon.'

'Perhaps it would be better if you wore the salmon,' Ruby tries, but she knows already that she has lost.

They are late getting to the parade. Eva resisted being left with Glenda, and even after Ruby had prised her tiny fingers from her blouse, and fled ruthlessly from her screams, there was still the matter of the gloves. On the way into the parade, she had pulled up outside David Jones and rushed through the ground floor to Accessories, leaving Granny Jenkins in the car with the engine still running.

'Don't expect me to pay for the parking fine,' Granny declared.

Miraculously, there was a single pair left. Ruby told the attendant not to bother wrapping them, and returned triumphantly to the car.

'An early Christmas present,' she said to Granny, who pulled them onto her stout fingers without a word of thanks.

Now, in the dressing room, Ruby hastily freshens up.

'A lady should never be seen to rush,' says the exquisite Mrs Shmith. But then she offers a nod of approval. 'Very polished indeed.'

Before Ruby has time to absorb this compliment, the girls begin stepping out in alphabetical order, and now it is her turn. *Very polished indeed*, she reminds herself as she slides out onto the catwalk. She feels a collective intake of breath; the atmosphere contracts, and fixes her there, under those lights. After a moment, the rehearsed moves unfold of their own accord. *Five strides towards the front, turn, then pause. Lead with the legs, body weight follows. Forward foot pauses; maintain discipline of the torso at all times.* She catches the eye of a young man in the audience and his face softens, and she rests for a moment in his regard. *Two steps to the right, then pivot. Heel a split second before the toe.* There are a few sharp points in the audience, a few small jags. There are always going to be some jealous girls, and she can hear Granny Jenkins coughing as if she has the plague. She knows she will pay for this moment, but that doesn't matter. It has been worth it. If only Arthur could have been here to photograph her. She doesn't even feel vanity, just rightness. She should be admired, and now she is.

At home that night, she serves dinner to her family with a gentle condescension.

Eva tips her milk into the mashed potato. 'Ma!' she says, gesturing at the empty cup.

Arthur has not yet asked about the parade.

'How was work today, Arthur?' asks Granny Jenkins.

'Grim, Mother. These are difficult times.'

Ruby wishes her resentment away.

'Uh-oh!' warns Eva, and drops her cup on the ground.

'That's enough!' Ruby's voice has too sharp an edge, and the family finishes its meal in silence.

Finally, Arthur leans back in his chair, turning his attention towards her. 'You're looking particularly well tonight, my dear.'

Ruby feels so grateful she could cry.

'Didn't you have something on today? A parade of some sort?'

'That's right,' Granny jumps in, before Ruby has a chance to respond. 'And there were some *lovely* girls, weren't there, Ruby? Girls of *true elegance and poise*, such as you have never seen the likes.'

Arthur chortles. 'Wouldn't have minded getting a load of that!'

At the end of the parade, Mrs Shmith had singled Ruby out for commendation, and offered her a place in the advanced course. It was a great honour, of course, but she realises now she will not be accepting it.

The secret to a graceful exit is a light gait. Judgemental thoughts ruin the complexion. Ruby eases herself to the edge of her seat, rises in a single vertical movement, and clears the table with smoothness and grace.

6

Glenda claims the day her youngest started school was the best day of her life, and that she had cracked open a bottle of champagne to celebrate.

'Dear gracious me,' says Ruby, into the telephone.

She doesn't go in for that type of gesture herself, and doubts that Glenda does either, in reality.

'I had my life back,' her neighbour explains.

But what is that life?

Ruby is not sure if she has uttered these words, or just thought them.

'I beg your pardon?'

'What can I bring on Saturday?'

'Darling, I've told you before that George would divorce me for one of your fruitcakes. And be sure to warn Arthur that George has revenge on his mind. He's been up early, practising his serve.'

Some sort of response is required, but Ruby can't think what it is.

'For heaven's sake, don't mope around,' exclaims Glenda. 'What are your plans? Do something wonderful. Get your hair done. Take a lover!'

Ruby has to laugh. Even if she were not in this condition, a lover would be the last thing on her mind. It is strange now to remember the early days of their marriage, the way she savoured Arthur's body. Studied every inch of it. His dense upper thighs; his tapering calves; his plate-like feet, which he jokingly referred to as his *large under-standing*. The loose pattern of hair on his torso, directing the eye downward to his touching, earnest sex. He kept the book on married love in his bedside cabinet, and together they managed to get the whole thing working very nicely. *Everyone possessing the least athletic training – i.e. the majority of people – will easily comprehend the need for exhalation during orgasm.* It was a revelation to Ruby: that such pleasure was available. Sometimes, when they visited the farm, she wondered whether Mother could guess just by looking at them – though she doubted Mother knew what an orgasm was; and even if she did, she certainly would never have been so rude as to have one.

Then along came Eva, long and golden and covered in down. A seal pup in her arms.

Of course, she continued to submit to Arthur's attentions, but they became another thing to get through. Monday was Washing Day; Tuesday was Ironing Day; Sunday was Love-making Day. It was a necessary duty like any other, yet somehow less satisfying without a pile of starched linen to show for it.

When she hangs up the phone, she is unnerved by the silence, and distracts herself with a series of large tasks she should not be doing in her condition. Arthur still hasn't got around to the pruning, so she does it herself, bumping the wheelbarrow against her swollen belly on the way to the compost. As if to show him, or the baby, or someone.

It is only when she passes the incinerator and sees Eva's small batch of mud cakes that she realises what she should be doing. She should be baking. Eva would surely welcome her at school if she brought a cake.

Sometimes, when Ruby makes a fruitcake, she soaks the dried fruit in a little brandy first, the way Mother would if she was in a forgiving mood. She doesn't tell Arthur, because it would only cause him to fret – at the risk to health, or the expense – and she couldn't be bothered explaining that the alcohol cooks off and just makes for a richer cake.

But now she realises she forgot to replace the brandy after the incident. To think that Granny Jenkins might have poked around on her last visit, and noticed it missing! Thank heavens for small mercies.

Absently, she switches on the wireless.

Girls and boys come out to play.

And the voice of Anne Dreyer: *Good morning, children.*

For once, nobody replies *good morning*, but apart from that, Eva might still be lying on her back behind the couch, singing to herself and quietly chattering.

Clickety-clunk, a-lunk-a-lunk, the train is coming, a-chunk-a-chunk.

It fills the large silence anyway, and provides a rhythm for her baking. At the end of the program Anne Dreyer says *goodbye now, children*, and Ruby feels a fleeting shame. She switches off the wireless and tidies herself up for school.

It is a curious thing to walk down a street without a child. You can go a lot faster, even when loaded down with a fruitcake. Unless you slow at the bottlebrush tree at the corner and finger its soft baby leaves. *Just like velvet.* It was Eva's favourite tree, and had been one of her first big words. *Bot-tle-brush.* She always took meticulous care arranging the consonants in her mouth.

When she arrives at school, Ruby takes a seat under the peppercorn tree, and as soon as the children are released for lunch Eva runs up and catapults herself into her lap.

'Mummy's going to have a baby,' she announces.

'Hush, darling,' Ruby says, smoothing the back of her daughter's hair. 'Nobody needs to hear about that.'

'Imagine if you was very old and just about to die and you turned into a baby. Only the Tooth Fairy could do that. Does she have a wand?'

'I'm not sure. How was your first morning?'

'Good thanks.'

She has traces of paint on her fingertips in bright primary colours: red, blue, yellow. How casually your children betray you. How quickly they belong to someone else.

'Now, my darling, would you like some cake?'

'No thanks Mummy. Can I please be accused?'

'But I thought you'd like a treat.' Absurdly, Ruby's eyes fill with tears. 'I baked a cake for you to share with your new friends.'

'I don't want cake thank you Mummy I love you.'

And so she releases her daughter, who hurtles to the playground. Then she wraps the unwanted cake in its tea towel, places it in her basket, and lets herself out of the school gate.

Usually Ruby prefers the week to the weekend. There is comfort in the fact of all the husbands packed into their offices, of the wives and babies in their modern homes. Everyone in their rightful place, guaranteeing the safe stewardship of the world. This, after all, is what they had fought for.

But today the footpaths are so empty that the whole suburb might have lost its children. How was this allowed to happen? Where is the Rumpelstiltskin with whom she made this pact?

A baby cries out from the tree above her, and she looks up in alarm – but it is only a blue-black crow, splendid and tyrannical.

She wouldn't have mentioned the pregnancy to Eva at all, except that Granny Jenkins had somehow sniffed it out.

'At it again, were we?' she had asked. 'At your age!'

'For heaven's sake,' Ruby had snapped. 'I'm all of thirty-two.' *It's not my doing*, she should have said. *Speak to your son about it.*

Anyway, who was Granny Jenkins to talk, given that she was on the wrong side of forty by the time Dolores came along?

'I thought Walter finished off on my abdomen,' Granny had

once told her, as Ruby peeled apples for a crumble. 'That's what Mrs Wilkinson said Mr Wilkinson did. I just assumed all the husbands knew to do that.'

Fancy saying that! Fancy speaking that way to a daughter-in-law, and in the kitchen!

There is a thought that keeps bobbing up that Ruby cannot afford to have. It concerns Granny Jenkins' shame at her own late pregnancy, and the measures she likely took to end it. It concerns all the ways in which Dolores is not quite right.

When Ruby pushes open the hotel door, she is disorientated at first by the darkness, but then she recognises the smell of Father after a harvest – tobacco and perspiration and beer – and it gives her the courage to approach the bar.

'What can I do for you, love?' asks the barman.

'I'm looking for the bottle department.'

'That right, love? Any bottle in particular?'

There is a lone man sitting at the bar, staring into his drink. He does not acknowledge her, but she does not need to see his face to know what he is. It is not just the stink of alcohol, but something besides: the rancid odour of his scalp, the encrusted dirt behind his ears. The smell of a man with no woman to care for him.

'A bottle of brandy, please.'

'Hold ya horses, sweetheart. Be right back.'

The man on the stool clears his throat. 'What's in the basket, missus?'

He turns to her and she flinches to see he is missing an eye. There is a terrible intimacy to that glistening pink socket.

'Fruitcake.'

'I like a bit of fruitcake meself.'

Sometimes Ruby makes accommodations for Arthur in her head, as if he had been damaged, somehow, by the war. But it is important to remember that he is no down-and-out. He is a fine, upstanding man, who thoroughly fulfils his responsibilities as husband and father.

'Always was partial to a slice of cake.'

'Were you just.'

'Always was keen on a piece of cake.'

Ruby is tired of carting the damn thing around anyway, heavy as a need. She swings it out of its basket and onto the counter.

'For goodness sake, take it then!' Her voice is harsher than she intends; the poor old boy has probably not had cake in years.

'Everything all right there, miss?' asks the barman, returning with the brandy.

The cake sits stolidly upon the bar, wrapped in Ruby's second-favourite tea towel. The man has made no move to claim it.

'Fine, thank you very much.'

There is no dignified way to retrieve her tea towel, so she just pays for the brandy and leaves.

At home, she replaces the bottle in the chiffonier, and hurries to the bathroom to wash her hands. In the mirror, she sees that the mascara has pooled around her eyes in two dark bruises, and realises she has been crying.

The shame of it is that she had taken extra care with her make-up this morning before going in to see Eva. She had sought to make herself beautiful for her daughter – as if she was meeting a lover.

It was a Friday when she found out. It had been a difficult few weeks at home, with Granny Jenkins visiting and generally making a nuisance of herself.

Ruby's heart sank at the sight of the doctor's smile.

'Good news, Mrs Jenkins. God has been kind to you and your husband a second time.'

For some moments afterwards she could not stand up. How had this been allowed to happen?

She remembered that night when she had left her dia-phragm to air-dry in the bathroom and forgotten about it entirely. The following evening she had found Eva playing with it in the bath, wedging the plastic cap – stretched to the point of transparency – on and off her bony knee.

'Look Mummy! A *knee* cap!'

She had whisked it away – *Not for children!* – and waltzed out of the room before there could be any further questions.

Is that all it took? A single moment of carelessness?

'Wonderful news,' she said to the doctor.

But she had her Eva. There was no need for any more babies.

If she never returned to that doctor, nobody would ever know.

Back at home, she knew exactly what to do: Isla had told her during the war. She placed a tureen of water on the boil and ran a bath. Then she returned to the kitchen, carried the tureen carefully into the bathroom, poured it into the tub, and repeated the process. She didn't keep gin in the house, but she had a bottle of brandy in the chiffonier, which was surely a good enough substitute.

As she slipped into the bath, there was a loud thud from her shocked heart, and her skin puckered away from the heat, but she slid down further until her torso was submerged and her breasts bobbed to the surface. She covered them with a flannel out of modesty, and then sipped at the brandy until the heat became bearable and finally almost pleasant. Her limbs were heavy; there were sparkles in the air. She might have been a fruitcake herself, marinating in brandy, dense and rich. It was not murder, after all, just a belated contraception.

Afterwards, she had just enough wit to hide the empty bottle amongst the preserving jars, and take herself upstairs to bed.

She woke to Arthur's concerned face hovering above her.

'Scrambled eggs for tea tonight,' she offered brightly.

His brow remained furrowed. If he detected the smell, he didn't mention a thing.

At school that afternoon, a couple of mothers are nattering away outside Eva's classroom. Young mothers, with that gloss on them – that unearned confidence – of those who hadn't properly known the war.

And the shop attendant said well my dear she said why don't you come back when you're twenty-one – when you're twenty-one she said! – and I'll be pleased to fix you up with some of our lotion. I didn't mention that I am well and truly into my mid-twenties and that little Susie was waiting out front with Mother.

Ruby pushes past them to the classroom window, leaning in to search for her daughter.

And suddenly a lot of things make sense – the looks I get when I'm out and about with little Susie for instance.

She scans the rows of desks for the specifics of her child: the cocky tilt of head, that peach-fuzz hair. Her heart is pounding, but she is not sure what it is that she fears.

As if I'm – forgive me for saying it ladies – but as if I'm some unfortunate girl.

There she is. Her head resting on her desk. Thumb in her mouth. Fast asleep. Still a baby, after all.

She lets herself into the classroom, entirely vindicated, ignoring the young mothers – *I really don't think you should –* to reclaim her child. As she picks her up, Eva stirs slightly and then fastens to Ruby's body; she is the exact same weight she was this morning, before she started school. Ruby shoots the distracted teacher a reproving glance and carries her baby outside.

My Susie would never fall asleep in the classroom, she hears, *she just has too much pluck.* But she moves away from the other mothers, back to the bench beneath the peppercorn tree.

The voices of other people's children carry over from the oval; her own child is warm in her lap. A magpie chortles above them, and she picks out the discreet smells of her baby: the burnt sugar of her hair, the tender scent of her scalp. By knowing her she may be able to keep her. As the afternoon sun beats down, the girl's hair becomes warm and a little stiff in her fingers, like spun gold. Soon the bell will ring, and Eva will startle awake and spring off her mother's lap before anyone sees her there. But now, her thumb is jammed into her mouth, and for once Ruby is not tempted to remove it. Instead, she takes the child's other hand in her own, spits on her handkerchief and washes the limp fingers one by one, removing all traces of paint.

7

Arthur was always very fond of his sister, and the whole thing is a very great tragedy, but it is hardly reason enough to move back to Adelaide. His parents still have each other, after all, and Ruby firmly believes it is in his best interests to remain as far away from his mother as possible. So whenever the subject comes up, she urges him to give due consideration to his career prospects, which are surely much greater on the eastern seaboard. But then they return home for Daisy's wedding, and everybody is so taken with baby Charlie, and Eva makes such a splash, that she begins to reconsider. Their cottage in Flemington, though pleasant enough, is hardly their dream home; and while the neighbours have made them very welcome, it is not the same as being around old friends.

Then, almost as if the gods are conspiring, Florence gets wind that they are in town, and invites them out to the new Maison de Danse. Ruby accepts with alacrity. She has made a new cloak for Daisy's wedding, of metallic teal with an artfully concealed pocket, which would benefit from a second outing. It would certainly not hurt to bring a little Melbourne style to her old Adelaide set.

When they arrive, she sees that Mavis and Bill Clarkson are once more in the thick of it.

'Ruby, you look so chic!' says Mavis. 'What do they say? *A woman can never be too rich or too thin.*'

'I'm not convinced about the *never too thin* part of that equation,' grumbles Arthur. 'Ruby's not half the woman she used to be.'

'No risk of being too rich,' she retorts.

Mavis, on the other hand, has become stout, while Bill looks much the same, apart from a sprinkling of salt and pepper in his hair. Unlike Arthur, he is not the sort to become more distinguished with age. There is still that appeal in his eyes, that urgent need for approval which does not quite become a man.

'Sweet Ruby Rose, might I have the first dance?'

She can see from the expressions of the other wives that Bill has worked his magic on them, and is determined this time not to fall under his spell. After all, she is older and wiser now, and has two children to her name. She has even lived in Melbourne. At the same time it is a great pleasure to dance with him, she will grant him that. It is better even than she remembered – he is careful yet relaxed, and authoritative in the way he handles her – and soon enough she finds herself telling him things.

It all starts with Mother's new Vauxhall. *The pinnacle of style,* Bill agrees, describing it in a way that sounds something like Mother herself. *Elegant and practical, upright yet not uncomplicated.* Perhaps it is this that allows her to get too comfortable. All at once she is telling him about Father's new position as farm manager for Daisy and Alexander, and how glad she is that Mother is finally able to have something nice for herself.

'Didn't your old man take proper care of her before?'

She knows this is no way to talk about a father, and yet there is something about the momentum of the dance that prompts her to keep talking.

'Bit of a naughty boy, my father. Always had a larrikin streak.'

Heavens! What is she doing? She has never even said as much to Arthur.

'Doesn't mind a bet, I recall you saying.'

It disarms her that he remembers. That last conversation was more than a decade ago – though she could likely recite it verbatim. What strikes her now is his energy. She feels it as they dance: they have a similar tempo. She never sits down and suspects he doesn't either. The jazz waltz gives way to the jitterbug gives way to the foxtrot, until it is getting to the stage where they have probably danced too much, but they continue to dance and she continues to talk. Before she knows it, she is describing how tirelessly Mother worked with the fowls, thinking that when they sold the farm she would be sitting on a nice little thing, and how she had nearly fainted when the bank manager said there were no savings.

'She'd gathered her earnings and sent Father to town to invest them, and I think he stayed at the Southern Cross Hotel. Probably met up with some of his old boys from St Peter's.'

'Fast crowd, that one,' says Bill. 'Mavis's father and his ilk. What's the bet he got into a poker school.'

'Woke up in the morning and didn't have any money left.'

'Poor devil.'

'What you might call a *loveable rogue.*'

Bill looks serious. 'Still. No place for secrets like that in a marriage.'

Perhaps it is this that brings her to her senses. She glances towards their table and sees that Arthur is looking fretful. Mavis is engrossed in conversation with Florence, but even her poise has become a little strained. Bill must have spotted it too, because at the end of that number he lets go of her hand. She thinks it is reluctantly, but cannot be sure.

'You're all aglow,' Arthur observes, when she joins him.

'I should hope so. My husband insists that ladies don't perspire.'

He laughs more loudly than is warranted, as she fishes around in her clutch for her compact. *Drat.* She had been so proud of her cape's concealed pocket that she had stored it in there. It is a shame to abandon Arthur at his most vulnerable, but she can hardly be expected to remain at the table with a shiny complexion. So she takes his hand and squeezes it twice – a code she has taught him that all is well – and makes her way back to the cloakroom.

As soon as the attendant shuts the door, she is comforted by the silence, and by this small, fur-packed room itself, redolent of perfume and hair oil and ancient body odour. She spots her cape immediately, more than holding its own amongst the tired-looking stoles, and retrieves her compact. As she leans into the mirror to blot her nose, she notices her hairpiece is askew. She has just started to unpin it, and is holding a tendril of hair in her hand – curled like the frond of a monkey-tail fern – when the attendant again opens the door.

And there is Bill, standing behind her in the mirror.

She feels exposed, with her hair half undone and her mirror face revealed: those intimate corrections of puckered lips and sucked-in cheeks.

Neither is his face quite as she knows it: his hair parted on the right instead of the left; that tiny birthmark displaced to the opposite cheek.

They make a handsome couple, she notes, and suppresses the thought.

She can still feel the imprint of his arm on her back, the weight of his hand in her own. As she swivels around to gaze at him in the flesh she feels something like awe. At his aliveness. At their existence in this cloakroom together, outside space, outside time.

He has a high colour from dancing, and his Brylcreemed hair is dark with perspiration. But his eyes, which are usually laughing, tell a different story.

They look wounded, somehow.

He neither advances towards her nor turns away.

Nor does she glance away, though it would clearly be proper.

She has never quite believed in falling in love. Surely it is a decision rather than an accident. A dive, rather than a fall.

But it is some sort of congress, this overlong eye contact.

It is almost too much, like looking into the sun. It is a look that promises something. But it is less summons than acknowledgement.

Of what?

That they are two mute animals, staring at one another from behind the bars of their cages.

She is not sure how long this continues, but at some point she realises there is a strand of hair between her fingers, and she pins it behind her ear. *I best be getting back*, he says at the same time, and the heavy door shuts behind him like an exhalation.

It is difficult to fix a hairpiece with a trembling hand. She will tell Arthur she has a headache, that they need to leave early. But by the time she returns to the table, Bill and Mavis have already gone.

Back in Melbourne, Ruby busies herself with the spring cleaning. She has only just bought the paint to freshen up the dining room when Arthur surprises her with news of a transfer to Adelaide, effective the following month.

She feels a great flood of something: hope or dismay, she is not sure which.

'Heavens,' she says, sitting down.

'No doubt it's a shock, dear, with all the work you've been doing around the house and so forth. But surely it can't entirely be a surprise.'

She reassures him that she is quite all right, and just needs a glass of water.

In fact she feels vertiginous, as if hurled into motion.

Unaccountably, she is reminded of the orrery in the McInernays' parlour. Once or twice Bobby had wound it for her, and she had been captivated by the movement of the planets, their steady trajectories as they rotated past one another and then came into alignment, dictated by any number of hidden levers and mechanisms. She supposes this is what they call fate; she supposes there is no option but to surrender.

PART TWO

1

Although Dolores has been gone for the better part of a year, the smell of urine lingers on in her rooms, regardless of how hard Ruby scrubs. Of course there is no ventilation, as Granny has a set against fresh air, and the entire arrangement – with the flat built into the rear of the house – seems to have been designed to keep Dolores shielded from public view. Ruby is keen to get them out of there as quickly as possible, and once Eva starts at the local school she applies herself vigorously to house-hunting. Over the weeks that follow, she compiles scrapbook upon scrapbook of clippings of open inspections, driving around Adelaide with Charlie in a Moses basket beside her. Naturally, Granny is a fount of advice. *Don't be fussy. Just buy and sell and you'll turn a profit, and one day you might be able to afford a Studebaker too.* Ruby is still not interested in a Studebaker; she wants only to find their dream home. *She's got tabs on herself, your wife,* Granny tells Arthur. *Airs and graces. Thinks she's royalty. Too good for any proper normal home.* But the longer it takes, the more resolute she becomes.

'Have you made contact with the old gang?' Arthur asks, one night over dinner. 'Surely it's time to alert them. Return of the prodigals and all that.'

Of course Ruby had been planning to get around to it, but there was always something to stop her. And now it has been three months.

Take a moment to cultivate poise before using the telephone, Mrs Shmith had advised, but the following morning, when Ruby sits down at the bench to phone Florence, her finger shakes so much in the rotary dial that she has to hang up and start again.

Florence answers immediately. 'What a glorious surprise. But goodness, I'm in danger of getting whiplash.'

'What do you mean?'

'Everyone's coming or going, it seems. I can't tell if I'm Arthur or Martha.'

'Who else, dear?'

'You must have heard about the Clarksons.'

'What?'

'They're off to Darwin, of all places. Apparently Bill's going to be quite the Grand Poobah. I can't imagine we'll be seeing them again in a hurry.'

For a moment, Ruby cannot quite remember how to talk.

'When are they leaving?' she manages, finally.

'Why, they left last week! We had the most wonderful shin-dig. Had I known you were back, I'd have invited the two of you.'

After Ruby hangs up, she remains sitting for a long time. At some stage, the baby starts crying; eventually she goes to pick him up.

*

Every house Ruby inspects thereafter threatens a life of misery. She has no interest in dank, dark bungalows, but equally lacks enthusiasm for cream-brick 'modern homes'. Perhaps Granny is right and she does needs to lower her standards, but the house-hunt has assumed a greater urgency. In desperation, she tries a new agent, a Mr Frogley, whom she has previously avoided on account of his blustery manner and ostentatious moustache. To her surprise he reveals something of a nose for quality, and after regretfully showing her yet another substandard property on the Parade, he mentions a Queen Anne–revival villa on Greenhill Road that belongs to the Bryce dry-cleaning family, and might soon be on the market. It was built in 1910 by the senior Mr Bryce for his wife, on a substantial corner block directly across from Hazelwood Park. The house is well beyond Ruby's price range, but since they are driving past anyway he suggests he might just knock on the front door and ask whether a quick inspection is possible.

As soon as they park outside, and Ruby glances down the slate pathway to the grand front verandah, all the items in her scrapbook – effective insulation, north-facing windows, price range – fall away. She doesn't even have to get out of the car to know. When Mr Frogley returns to escort her to the door, the housekeeper explains that the lady of the house is resting but happy for them to have a look. And Ruby steps inside and gazes into that vast passage that travels all the way down to the back, and knows she has stepped into her life, and she is home.

*

'You're looking very comely tonight,' observes Arthur, as she pours his burgundy. She has indeed taken special care with her make-up, and changed into his favourite blouse with the lace trim. 'Seems that house-hunting suits you. Though I wouldn't advise you to draw it out.'

She laughs, and brings in Eva for her goodnight kiss.

'I don't want to go to bed,' laments the child. 'Because I have a headache. It's not a normal headache but a really terrible one. My head just invented it.'

'That's the worst news I've heard all day,' commiserates Arthur, pulling her onto his lap.

'It might go on for two years or until I'm dead or one week.'

'How about I give you a kiss. Better?'

She nods, skipping off his lap and out of the room.

'Too clever by half, that one,' he says. 'Could even go on to have a career.'

Dinner is, of course, insufferable, with Granny demanding to know why Ruby hasn't yet found a house. *Can't stay here forever, you know. Those children are a strain on my nervous system.* Ruby flees to the kitchen to do the dishes, but even here there is no escaping Granny's voice. *Thinks she's Lady Muck, your wife. Not so much as lifting a finger to find you a house. Knows when she's on to a good thing, she does.*

Back in their quarters, Arthur announces he wishes to have a word. Ruby brings him a port, then sits on the little footstool by his chair, easing his fine broad foot out of his loafer and onto her lap.

He clears his throat. 'I know we've been perfectly comfortable here, and that Mother has made us very welcome. But, my dear, it cannot go on indefinitely.'

A welcome opening indeed. 'As it happens I saw a house today that might be just the ticket.'

'How much are they asking for?'

She presses down on the grooves between his toes. 'It's one of those Queen Anne villas I know you love. Set across Greenhill Road from Hazelwood Park, right there by the tennis courts.'

'Hazelwood Park! Surely that's well beyond us.'

She knows he has spent hours poring over charts at the dining table, contemplating deposits and interest rates and projected repayments. What he cannot be expected to realise is that this is no longer relevant; everything has been superseded by a larger claim.

But one must be strategic when addressing a husband.

'I realise finances are your domain, dear. But I've given some thought to how we might afford it. We could readily accommodate a boarder with a restoration of the stables.'

'A boarder? In our own home?' His socked foot clenches beneath her hands. 'Restoration wouldn't be cheap, you know.'

'I wouldn't want you to worry about that.' She moves her hands up to his calves, and kneads with some fervour. 'I'd oversee all the practicalities, and I've given some thought to home economies.'

He snorts. 'To be quite frank, all this talk of boarders and home economies worries me enormously. All I'm after is a *proper, normal home*. Can it really be so hard?'

She continues kneading, though it has become something of an effort.

'The point is that I don't want us to struggle. I'm sorry, darling, but we have to aim within our reach.'

He pats her on the head, signalling that the conversation is over; she abandons the massage and stares at the carpet. Then, like a sleepwalker, she moves to the liquor cabinet to refill his glass.

'Tell me about the house then,' he says with a sigh.

She starts by telling him about the wide jarrah passage leading all the way down to the back door; and about the master bedroom with its box bay window and window seat; and about the dear side porch that would make a wonderful sunroom. Then she gets to the leadlight features and the ornate ceilings and the wide verandah and even the original maids' bells. It is more than she means to say, but she finds she cannot stop, and soon she is outlining her vision for the garden: the fernery she will establish out the back; the hydrangeas that will flourish down the side; the golden elm she will plant alongside the fishpond.

'I see.' He takes a sip of his port. 'And would it make you happy?'

It seems to her that if she had this house – this one thing – it would allow her to give him everything else.

'It would, darling.'

He takes her hand, which he contemplates for some time. And then – beloved man – he suggests that the two of them might go and see it together.

*

Although Granny had not wanted them to stay, she is now staunchly opposed to them leaving, finding much to fault in the new house and advising them to subdivide it and rent it out. But it has become easier for Ruby to be gracious to the older woman, and she moves through her remaining days in Henley Beach in a spirit of *noblesse oblige*.

'Our new house is a mansion,' says Eva. 'We're going to be *rich*.'

'Poor as church mice, more like it,' says Granny. 'It's going to cost you a fortune to keep it warm.'

The day before the move, as Ruby is boxing up some final items, she hears a sudden kerfuffle from the neighbouring rooms. Charlie jerks awake with an indignant shout; she ignores him and rushes into the parlour, where she finds Granny shrieking.

'Answer me, Walter!'

Ruby has never previously seen a corpse, but it is immediately clear that Grandpa Jenkins has become one. He is sitting in his chair with his eyes half open, looking almost indolent.

'Walter, pay me heed!' The gist of Granny's loud complaint seems to be that she is not getting the attention that is her due. 'For goodness sake, girl!' she says, catching sight of Ruby. 'Don't just stand there gawking. Fetch the brandy and *revive* the man!'

But at that very moment Ruby hears a brutal thump from the baby's room, followed by a howl: Charlie must have climbed from his cot and fallen. And her fateful decision is to tend to her child rather than attempt to resuscitate a deceased father-in-law, who at any rate looks quite comfortable, and would likely prefer to remain *in absentia*.

After she has collected the baby, she pours Granny a snifter of brandy and leads her into her bedroom. Then she calls Arthur at work. She doesn't have the heart to leave Grandpa all alone in the parlour, so she changes Charlie on the rug in front of the heater, and then – because it wouldn't do for Arthur to see his father in such a state – she gently closes the old man's eyelids. It is a more intimate transaction than any she shared with him when he was alive, the skin as soft and tenderly wrinkled as the child's scrotum she has just wiped clean.

When Arthur arrives home, Granny explains that it was all Ruby's fault, because she had failed to fetch the brandy. And that no option remains but for Granny to move into the new house with the four of them.

'I wish you wouldn't,' says Ruby, reflexively.

'It's my son's house and you can't stop me,' replies Granny, and indeed nobody ever does.

2

Ruby's first big job in the new house is to hose the calcimine off the inside walls. She summons Daisy, who has still failed to conceive and seems grateful for the distraction, and she and Mother come up for a week, bringing an extra-long hose from the farm. The three of them squirt at the walls, and sweep them with a broom, and hack at them with a paint scraper, until all that remains is the plaster itself, a blank slate for the family's future life. Eva and Charlie cavort joyfully through the chalky mess, but Arthur becomes fretful, so Ruby ensures she has a functional kitchen at all times, and is diligent with her apple crumbles. When she gets around to the painting, it brightens the place no end; the eggshell walls are so fresh against the jarrah floors that she is reluctant to hang her tapestries. At night, she props open the doors so that the gully breeze rushes down the long hallway to dry the paint. It feels almost as if the house itself were breathing.

'You're not out on the farm anymore,' Arthur chides her. 'We're in the big smoke, and crime is rampant.'

Ruby has sometimes wondered if there are two types of men: those enlarged by the war, and those who were not. It is not only about *derring-do* but something else besides. A man's relationship to the physical world, perhaps. Arthur soon becomes fixated upon the risk of electrocution, bringing home a rubber mat to place beneath the ironing board, and insisting Ruby wear rubber thongs whilst operating the Mixmaster. It is clear she needs to settle him in properly before she can even think of anything else, so she asks Father to come down for the weekend and build him a bookcase. Of course he does a lovely job of it, with the keenest of lines and most immaculate of joinery, and before he knows it, Arthur is set up in a reading nook, with his armchair and foot rest and the tasselled lamp they brought over from Melbourne. As long as Ruby serves dinner at the regular time, and avoids climbing ladders within his line of sight, she can work as hard as she likes.

Naturally, Granny Jenkins doesn't lift a finger to help, despite making regular appearances to discuss the renovations of her quarters. Usually she announces her presence with a show of such coughing and spluttering that Ruby is forced to climb down from her ladder and make her a cup of tea, even if busily occupied with a cornice. Granny obviously expects special treatment as a widow, and has taken to dressing entirely in black, which does her no favours and makes her very drack and dreary indeed. Mercifully, she keeps changing her mind about the renovations, which postpones the inevitable, but eventually she settles upon a plan to divide the rumpus room into her own bedroom, kitchen and bathroom. She demands that her front door opens directly onto Ruby's kitchen – *Need to keep an eye on what's what* – but Ruby puts her foot down at this, insisting that the door must instead be at the far end of the hallway. A serious border skirmish develops, and several times Arthur recommends surrender, but the last thing Ruby wants is Granny breathing down her neck every time she makes a rice pudding, so she vehemently defends the principle that every woman deserves to be mistress of her own kitchen until Granny relents.

And at last she can turn her attention to the garden. Despite its good bones, it has suffered recently from neglect. Fortunately, Ruby knows exactly what needs to be done, and she moves through her jobs in a state of grace, as if taking dictation from on high. She plants the elm by the fishpond and two silver birches out the front; she sows sweet peas and poppies in the new curved beds; she cleans out the pond and populates it with plump goldfish. By the end of the year, the garden is producing capsicum, cucumbers, basil and sweetcorn, and the neighbours are stopping by frequently with compliments. Ruby has to pinch herself: that life could be this Edenic. She cannot imagine how she allowed herself to be so foolish last year in relation to Bill Clarkson. It was as if she had fancied herself a Scarlett O'Hara or something, when clearly all she ever required was a garden.

'You're not overdoing it, are you?' asks Arthur, if he returns home to find new garden beds dug over and pavers placed.

'Of course not.' Although camouflaged in house dress and pinny, Ruby knows she has become brown and wiry through work.

He glances mournfully at her dwindling bust. 'Mind you're getting enough nutrition, dear.'

Once the renovations are complete, and Granny moves in, Ruby congratulates herself on her foresight regarding the hallway. The moment she hears Granny's warning stomp on the floorboards, she puts out a Scotch Finger biscuit as decoy and hides evidence of whatever project she might be embarking upon. The one drawback to the layout is that Granny has first access to the back steps, and pops out of the screen door as soon as Arthur returns home to accost him with the day's grievances.

Your wife was out on the roof today cleaning the gutters. Your wife let the baby cry for a good half-hour this morning in his cot.

The only saving grace is that the old woman is a creature of habit. Each morning, she fetches the paper, because she *doesn't want anyone else to fade the print*. After reading it from cover to cover, she catches the bus into town, coming home in time to make a nuisance of herself as Ruby prepares dinner. Mercifully, she avoids the garden altogether, and Ruby spends more and more of her day out there. As she prunes the hedges or neatens the borders, she feels a pervasive sense of orderliness, the events of recent years not only forgotten, but disproved.

When Ruby discovers a mouse in the kitchen, she chooses not to mention it to Arthur, but discreetly sets a trap, removing its tiny cadaver early the following morning. But when Granny finds mouse droppings in her living room, nobody hears the end of it. *A plague of vermin is upon this house!* Arthur becomes so unsettled that Ruby picks up a tabby kitten from the local pet shop. Upon his return from work, he seizes the cat in delight, christening it 'Louis'; to Ruby's surprise, the animal takes up permanent residence in his reading nook, sitting proprietorially on his lap whenever he is at home.

Often, after school, Eva wheels little Charlie across the road to the park in her doll's pram. Of course Arthur worries about the children roaming unsupervised, but Ruby argues that they are always within cooee; as she gardens, she can usually make out their small figures in the distance, building dams or feeding the ducks. It is at the park, allegedly, that Charlie comes out with his first word: *duck*, pronounced with a self-satisfied *k* at the end, as if sealing the word from leakage. Soon enough nobody can stop him talking. *I taught him how to talk*, Eva explains. *And now we're working on arithmetic. He's making very expressive progress.* Shortly thereafter, Eva claims he has taken his first steps by the tennis courts, though there are no further witnesses to such a feat for some time.

One morning, when Granny has taken the bus to town, and Charlie is burbling to his toy cars in the dining room, Ruby prepares the oven for a batch of Anzac biscuits. The match dies in her hand, so she lights another, climbing in further to investigate.

Then a mighty *whoosh*, and blackness.

The next thing is the smell of singed hair: a dark, barbaric odour. And Charlie looming above her with a full nappy.

'Mummy cook Mummy.'

Gingerly, she stands up and then, despite some wooziness, takes him into the bathroom to change him.

'Not a single word to Daddy,' she instructs.

In the mirror, she sees that her eyebrows are burnt clear away; her inflamed face wears an expression of astonishment.

She soothes her skin with one of Daisy's homemade ointments, and carefully sketches her eyebrows back on with a brow pencil.

'A new style of make-up,' she explains to Arthur that evening. 'Very up-to-the-minute.'

'Always has to be a fashion plate,' laments Granny.

Over the months that follow, Ruby's eyebrows show no sign of growing back, but she still considers it a close escape. Never again will she climb into an oven with a lit match. She could have been hurt, or – almost as serious – Arthur might have found out.

By the following spring, the renovation of the stables is complete, and Ruby interviews her first boarder: a Mr Yang from Hong Kong. He explains that he is studying Medicine, and wishes to live in a house with children in order to practise his English. Although Ruby has had no previous dealings with the Chinese, she finds Mr Yang entirely amenable. To further recommend him, he is most taken with her Eva – *Your daughter is like an angel from heaven* – as if he has never before seen a child with fair hair.

I've always said Eva is the spitting image of Hayley Mills, says Granny, *do you know Hayley Mills, Mr Yang, the lovely child star?* – and launches into one of her blow-by-blow descriptions of *Tiger Bay*, which seems to last longer than any film. Once he has moved in, Granny persuades him to join her on her regular Saturday excursions to the pictures with her cousin, Primrose. The three of them make quite a sight: Mr Yang in his impeccable suit; Primrose as thin as a thread, with her red hennaed hair; and Granny in her best fur coat, never mind the weather, wielding her walking stick as a weapon. Ruby spares a thought for any recalcitrant ushers, but is always thankful for the reprieve, and Saturdays soon become her favourite day of the week, with Eva on hand to help with little Charlie, and Arthur at his most relaxed. After tennis in the park, followed by a nice warm bath, he installs himself in his armchair for the afternoon, and as long as Ruby finishes gardening in time to prepare a good roast, he could not be happier.

It is on one such idyllic Saturday afternoon that Ruby sends Eva over to the park to collect some grass clippings. To her chagrin, the child returns empty-handed.

'For heaven's sake, what have you done with my wheelbarrow?'

'I was getting the clippings,' Eva says, biting her lip as if she has wet the bed. 'And then a man rode up on a bike. He wanted to know if I knowed where a *fock* was. Sorry Mummy I couldn't really hear what he said because he had a very quiet voice and then he put his coat on the ground and said lie down and then I will show you a *fock*. I said beg your pardon like you said is good manners. Then he got angry and said he would make me and I felt scared so I runned away and I'm sorry I left the wheelbarrow.'

Even before the child has finished, Ruby has raced out the front gate with gardening fork in hand. It is a good thing there is no traffic on Greenhill Road at that moment because she looks neither left nor right but charges straight ahead with murderous purpose, and sure enough sees a youth loitering by the tennis courts, kicking around the grass clippings next to her abandoned wheelbarrow, and she runs towards him with a visitation of such speed and fury that it feels almost supernatural, and the moment he claps eyes upon her, rushing at him like a banshee scarecrow and roaring in some primal maternal tongue – *That anyone, ANYONE, would have the hide to look at my daughter like that* – he scampers onto his bike and pedals frantically away, but she pursues him past the ducks and picnicking families and tennis players, many of whom she no doubt knows from the neighbourhood, all the while brandishing her fork – *How DARE you, how DARE you, how DARE you!* – across the foot bridge and right to the other side of the park until he disappears from sight and is gone.

When she returns to the tennis courts, she discovers a duffel coat spread out upon the ground, like a parody of chivalry. She seizes the item, and could well rip it apart with her teeth, but instead she marches over to the bin and hurls it in. Then she fills the wheelbarrow with clippings, gently balances her fork across the top, and crosses the road to home.

Eva stands at the front fence, regarding her with awe.

'You did exactly the right thing to come and tell me,' Ruby says. She kneels in front of the child and takes her carefully by the hand. 'But you must never, ever, under any circumstances, mention a word of this to your father. Do you understand?'

Eva nods gravely, and returns to the sandpit to play.

3

When Eva is offered a scholarship to the Anglican Ladies' College, commended particularly for her arithmetic and her grammar, Ruby is as proud as can be, but of course she does not mention this to her daughter. Instead, she urges Eva to keep the news close to her chest. One should never draw attention to one's exceptionality; and besides, she fears scholarships smack of charity. She cannot abide the thought of the other parents looking down on them, particularly as she and Arthur had been planning to send Eva to the Ladies' College anyway.

But there is no denying that the scholarship is something of a windfall. Then, when Arthur receives a small promotion at work, she feels almost prosperous.

'About time,' she says. 'Everything you do for them. And us living off the smell of an oily rag.'

'It's always been quite a well-paying job, for all that,' he replies.

He is prompted to buy a television set for Granny, which at least keeps her out of trouble for the duration of *Pick a Box*, and then a record player for himself, housed in a very smart and modern walnut cabinet. Each night, upon returning home from work, he makes a beeline for the lounge room.

'An appointment with a certain Johann Sebastian,' he explains.

By the time Ruby brings in his port, he is listening to a Bach cantata, 'Ich Habe Genug', with Louis on his lap.

'I have enough,' he translates. And if she leans over and kisses him on the lips, he grins up at her. '*Ich habe mehr als genug.*'

It is on one such evening that Arthur makes the unprecedented suggestion that Ruby take a holiday.

'A holiday? From what?'

'From the myriad concerns of domestic life,' he says, although he does not actually mention Granny by name. 'And I suspect your mother might benefit from the same.'

It is true that Mother has been having a miserable time of late, with Father driving her to distraction with his drinking and general slovenliness, but Ruby has to think of the children, whom she can hardly abandon to Granny's housekeeping. But then Daisy offers to come and stay – *Can't think of a better holiday than a week with my favourite two* – and before she knows it, Ruby is driving Mother up to Mildura, where Arthur has booked them into the Grand Hotel. And he could scarcely have made a better choice – what with the well-appointed rooms, the attentive service and the sumptuous meals in the Chandelier Dining Room. Even Mother, a stern critic of buffet lunches, is impressed by the corned beef, and most particularly the artful use of cloves. She helps herself to seconds, prompting Ruby to do the same: Arthur will only be pleased if she comes home with more meat on her bones.

'How the other half lives,' Ruby observes.

'Better not get used to it,' Mother warns her, and yet already she looks less drawn.

When they return to their room, they see that someone has turned down the bed and arranged a small posy upon each of their pillows. It is a little unsettling at first – all this being tended to rather than tending – but it does not take very long to get used to. The bed itself is so comfortable, with its modern mattress and quilt, that lying in it feels like a type of embrace. It is almost as if the hotel itself were mothering them, and the two ladies sleep like queens.

The following morning, they take a cruise on the paddle steamer *Melbourne*. From the upper deck, Mother points out a pelican hunched in the water, its bill loaded with fish; Ruby draws her attention to a flotilla of ducks, moving purposefully towards the shore. Mother enquires after Ruby's fernery and then after the children, with Ruby reporting that the maidenhairs are thriving; that Eva looks a treat in her new school uniform; and that Charlie is forever tinkering away at the piano.

'Hope he practises his scales,' says Mother fretfully.

'After a fashion.'

What Ruby doesn't mention is that Eva has started giving her lip; and that there is always something around the house that needs to be fixed; and that she sometimes wonders whether life should be something more than a series of daily tasks, successfully dispatched.

'And how are you managing with that Mrs Jenkins?'

It is courteous of Mother to refer to her as 'Mrs Jenkins' rather than 'your mother-in-law', and yet Ruby still harbours a private shame. She cannot help but feel that Granny Jenkins reflects poorly upon her as mistress of the house: after six years of living beneath the same roof, she really ought to have found a way to lift the tone.

'Well enough, I suppose. Though she is never one to put herself out.'

'Quite,' says Mother. 'Mother was the same.'

'Oh?'

'Never did want me to be a nurse.'

This is something of a revelation, but before Ruby can pursue it further they are interrupted by a shriek from the loud-speaker, followed by the booming sound of the captain's voice.

Ladies and gentlemen, you will no doubt be interested to know that the boiler has a maximum steam pressure of one hundred and fifty pounds.

'Fascinating,' remarks Mother. 'You must remember to convey that to Arthur.'

Ruby suspects that Arthur wouldn't be the least bit interested – as opposed to someone like Bill Clarkson, for example. They pass a tree bedecked with cockatoos; when the racket subsides, Ruby observes that she never realised Mother wished to be a nurse.

'Indeed I did, dear, but you had to supply your own uni-form. And your grandmother just would not come to the party. Nor was she one for doing things *particularly*. When I think of the way she conducted herself.'

'And how was that?'

'Oh dear, you know the sort of thing. She would *hang* over the front fence to talk to the neighbour, for example, without an iota of shame.' She shudders a little. 'You can no doubt appre-ciate why I wished to move on.'

'What do you mean?'

'I accepted that position as lady's companion. In your father's family.'

'And then you met the young man himself,' Ruby offers, like the happy ending of a fairytale.

'Indeed,' says Mother, dourly. 'Of course, the neighbours warned me.'

'A good thing, on balance, that you ignored that warning.'

Mother gazes fatalistically at the approaching lock. 'I've made my bed. And I've learned to lie in it.'

As you will see, there are four steel gates into the lock chamber. There are four butterfly valves upstream, which are opened to fill the chamber, and then the water flows in through two tunnels.

'Your father would appreciate that information,' says Mother, and they do not speak of him again for the remainder of the holiday.

*

The following morning, on the recommendation of the lovely young woman at reception, they visit the Art Gallery, housed in a gracious villa with inlaid Italian tiles in the front passageway, and the most exquisite stained-glass windows from England. Even Mother is full of admiration, though Ruby suspects she would have preferred the villa with no art inside. She parks herself before an unthreatening Hans Heysen landscape, venturing no further, but Ruby moves through the rooms in a state of rapture, gazing shamelessly at the human form: the soulful, lovely face of Anna Pavlova; a Degas pastel of a woman's generous rump; a group of naked, muscular Anzacs, cavorting at sea like gods. They call to her, somehow; they clamour at her with their bodiliness. She would like to be holding someone's hand.

On such occasions, she wonders if Bill ever thinks of her too.

Only last week, Florence had mentioned that he and Mavis were expecting another child.

'Surely not!' Ruby had exclaimed.

'By all accounts they're thriving,' Florence responded, with the faintest note of reprimand, and Ruby had hastened to supply the appropriate noises.

Had she imagined he would not continue with his life, seven years after their last meeting?

But this notion that he could, and so readily.

After lunch, it is a relief to be installed in the hotel's rose garden, with the known quantity of a tea cup in her hand.

'And when I think of the way she acted towards Mr Hamester,' says Mother.

'Who?'

'Mother,' says Mother, as if there had been no gap in the conversation since yesterday morning.

'But who in heaven's name was Mr Hamester?' All week, Ruby feels she has been lagging behind her mother's revelations.

'A most desirable swain. The manager of the Eudunda Farmers. Whenever he came to spend the weekend, his horse and trap were always loaded to the hilt. But your grandmother was not remotely accommodating. One morning there was no butter in the pantry for his breakfast, but she wasn't the least bit concerned. Didn't turn a hair.'

Ruby draws Mother's attention to the peace rose: the way its delicate yellow yields to a sunset peach.

'We must count our blessings,' Mother agrees. 'It was a great relief to me that you, at least, found so suitable a husband.'

'That I did,' says Ruby.

Every evening before dinner, Ruby changes into one of her smart modern shifts, and Mother replaces her everyday petticoat with her best petticoat, and the two of them descend the staircase together. It is Ruby's favourite moment of the day: the approach to the Chandelier Dining Room, towards the low murmur of the other guests and the aroma of pea soup and roast lamb. *Always lead with your legs*, Mrs Shmith had advised, *and you will surely glide into a room.* And every evening, as she glides into the room, Ruby collects a swag of admiring glances;

but soon enough she finds herself sitting at the same table by the wall, watching Mother browse the *à la carte* menu, and then waiting for the soup to arrive. All of which is entirely pleasant, but does not quite add up to that feeling of promise, of a proximate other world.

On their final night in Mildura, after the remaining guests have retired to the drawing room for cards, the ladies linger over their wine trifles. Ruby notices Mother glancing at the piano in the corner – a white upright, shiny as a thoroughbred – and on a whim, suggests she might like to play something.

'Dear girl, I couldn't possibly.'

'It really would be a great treat for me.'

To her surprise, Mother shyly stands and takes a seat on the piano stool. And then there is that old, familiar transformation. When they were girls, Ruby and Daisy would sometimes steal into the parlour to watch Mother play. Seated at the piano, she bore no resemblance to the mother they knew by day – who fiercely stalked flies around the kitchen with the swat, insisting that children remained *in or out*, so that if you elected to play outside it became a binding day-long contract and you dared not open the screen door until dinner for fear of vexing her by letting in a fly. Then, as now, her rigorous hands revealed a surprising eloquence; her face, with its frown lines released, became the face of a younger, more hopeful stranger. Where did she go, at such moments? Which life was she living?

The waiter stops cleaning to applaud. 'Mozart?' he ventures.

Mother looks dismayed, as if she has waylaid part of herself.

'Schubert. Come along then, Ruby.'

Back in their room, after they have set aside their clothes for the trip homeward, and tucked themselves up in their beds, Ruby asks whatever became of Mr Hamester.

'He made a request that could not be countenanced,' Mother replies. Her voice is even more gravelly than usual, perhaps because she is lying down.

'You don't mean to say …?'

'Heavens no, he was entirely honourable in that way.'

She is silent for a very long while, but Ruby can tell from the sound of her breath that she is not yet asleep.

'It would seem the same could not be said for his sister,' she says finally. 'And Mr Hamester had this notion that he and I could, you might say, cover it up.'

'Goodness. A devoted brother, then.'

'Of course I couldn't even consider it. What would people think?'

She understands her mother's position, but it is a great sadness, really. That so much should have been sacrificed.

'Do you ever wonder what became of him?'

'I'm sure that's none of my business.'

Ruby has the strangest thought: that it would be a tremendous relief to say something about Bill. But what on earth would she say? That there was a moment, once, in which they had exchanged a look?

'The path not taken,' she suggests instead.

'It was not a true path for all that.'

'All turned out for the better then.'

'Bygones must be bygones. At the very least.'

From the passageway, Ruby can hear the voices of other guests returning to their rooms. *Beginner's luck, that was. Next time I'm dealing.* A man laughs and a woman shrieks – *Stop that, you scoundrel!* – and then a door is pulled shut.

The two of them lie silently on their twin beds. Finally Mother begins to snore.

r Yang returns from his annual holiday to Hong Kong with an immaculately tailored suit for himself, and a turquoise silk cheongsam for Ruby.

'Very nice indeed,' he says admiringly, when she models it. 'Fits you like a glove.'

'But how are you expected to do anything?' asks Eva. 'I'd prefer the suit.'

'Beauty is the wisdom of woman,' asserts Mr Yang, in his well-spoken way, and for once Eva has no smart-alecky rejoinder.

Ruby just has to marvel at the man. Now that he has started his surgical training, he has become in every way the Australian gentleman, and is such a keen student of table manners that Ruby could happily take him to Buckingham Palace – which is more than she could say about Granny Jenkins, forever talking with her mouth full, or using her fork as a scoop, shovelling peas onto the wrong side of the tines.

He produces a photograph of his fiancée, a Taiwanese actress. *Really quite famous*, he says shyly.

Looking at the photo, Ruby feels a small rush of aesthetic

pleasure. She is actually *moved* by the woman's beauty: by her symmetrical swooping brows, her petulant rosebud mouth. Even Eva expresses a grudging admiration, and Ruby hopes it might inspire her towards higher standards of personal grooming. Understandably, Mr Yang has cooled on the girl's hair, which is not washed as frequently as it ought to be, but he is more than happy for her to borrow his copy of *Grey's Anatomy*. Eva pores over it with an avidity that strikes Ruby as unladylike.

At the beginning of her intermediate year, Eva makes the extraordinary announcement that she wishes to be a doctor.

'Very respectable career,' says Mr Yang.

'It may be that Pharmacy is more appropriate for a woman,' suggests Arthur. 'More suitable to the demands of raising a family. That is, if you really have an interest in ailments and so forth.'

'I've no shortage of ailments if you like that sort of thing,' offers Granny. 'I'll show you rashes that will make your hair stand on end. But who in heaven's name would ever want to go to a *lady doctor*?'

Ruby is confounded by Eva's announcement, but Granny's words force her into a position. 'A doctor for a daughter, fancy that! Wouldn't that be something, Arthur?'

He finishes his mouthful and nods thoughtfully. 'We will of course support you in any profession you choose to pursue, my dear.'

*

Although the study of Chemistry is unprecedented at the Anglican Ladies' College, the headmistress generously assigns Miss Pickering, the senior Domestic Science mistress, to tutor Eva. And all seems to be going swimmingly, with Eva receiving an unbroken succession of A's, until the Intermediate public examination.

'The first question was about atomic number,' Eva rages over dinner. 'What the heck is atomic number?'

'Language, please,' chides Arthur. 'Your grandmother is at the table.'

Granny harrumphs, fanning herself with her napkin.

'Miss Pickering never mentioned a *thing* about atomic number. Stupid old fossil.'

Charlie hoots with laughter, almost falling off his chair.

'I'm sure it wasn't as bad as all that,' Ruby says.

'I'll never get into Medicine with that *dunce* of a teacher.'

Ruby is struck by how very plain her daughter looks, with that frowning face and that great mass of unwashed hair.

'Try not to be cross, dear. Rage spoils the complexion.'

The girl turns to her with a look of incomprehension verging on wonder.

'Mum, I don't give two hoots about my complexion. I just want to be a doctor.'

When the results of the state-wide examination are released, and Eva receives a C for Chemistry, it is clear that some sort of action is required. And so, with a sinking heart, Ruby makes an appointment to see Miss Pickering at the school; regrettably, Eva insists on coming too.

It is always such a pleasure to step into the college grounds, with those velveteen lawns and immaculate tennis courts, and that elegant new chapel – a tribute to good taste as much as faith. Why could Eva not simply go along with all of this? Why did she always have to make things more complicated?

Miss Pickering receives them in the staff room with a silver tea service. 'I'm terribly sorry, Mrs Jenkins,' she says, with a fetching frown. She has always struck Ruby as a woman of great cultivation, if a trifle on the mature side. 'I fear I let dear Eva down. I must accept full responsibility for not having read the syllabus correctly.'

'That's quite all right,' says Ruby, who is prepared to leave it at that. She does not serve Earl Grey at home, as bergamot disagrees with Arthur, but it is certainly a pleasure to be sitting on this chintz sofa, enjoying the tea's delicate taste.

However, Eva is not so readily soothed. 'Miss Pickering, do you even know what an atomic number is?'

'One does not look to a ladies' college for this sort of technical information,' Ruby reassures the teacher.

'I can certainly do my best to find out for you.'

'That would be a great kindness. My husband and I have frequently remarked upon the level of personal care at the college.'

'But Mum,' Eva says quietly. 'This is my future.'

Miss Pickering appears not to have heard Eva's words, and leans forward to refill Ruby's cup. Through the window, Ruby can hear the orderly *plonk* of a tennis ball, like a polite conversation. It would be the easiest thing to pretend she didn't hear

Eva either, and to remark amiably upon the early arrival of summer. But to her dismay, she has realised that her daughter cannot remain at the Ladies' College. She places the tea cup back on its saucer; its floral aroma disperses into the air. They will have to enrol her at the local public school, where she will miss out on countless refinements, but will at least enjoy the educational opportunities afforded to a young man. It is the last thing she would ever have wished for, and she knows Arthur will take some convincing, but as Miss Pickering continues to simper at them, blinking too rapidly, it is abundantly clear that they have no choice.

On the way home, Ruby urges Eva to tell anyone who asks that she is interested in Dentistry rather than Medicine, lest people think she is getting above her station.

Arthur takes the news better than Ruby might have expected – *A credit to the girl that she shows such commitment* – and it is certainly a feather in the headmaster's cap that he has captured a girl from the Ladies' College. But it does cause Ruby a pang to see Eva in that public school uniform, with its brash primary colours, and no gloves to boot. And she cannot help but worry about the more permissive standards of a co-educational institution, particularly when the girl is handful enough already.

In June, Ruby takes Mother on their now-annual holiday to Mildura. As usual, they are treated like royalty, returning home thoroughly replenished and ready to take on whatever is lying in wait. But no sooner have they pulled into the carport than

Granny ejects herself from the fly-screen door – *popping out like toast*, as Eva describes this manoeuvre, usually performed upon Arthur's return from work – and is hobbling over the cobblestones with a look of such urgent purpose that Ruby alights from the car even before Mother has had time to undo her seatbelt.

'Good heavens, Granny, whatever is the matter?'

The old woman's face is beetroot red, scrunched up in furious triumph.

'He's gone and got you a new refrigerator. He wanted it to be a surprise – *see!*'

Behind her, framed in the doorway, are the disappointed faces of Arthur, Daisy and the children. Sure enough, Arthur – advised by a coalition of Eva and Daisy – has purchased a brand-new refrigerator for Ruby's birthday, with two doors and its very own freezer compartment, in a modern shade of avocado. It is wrapped in a giant maroon bow, which complements the avocado beautifully – she recognises Daisy's eye immediately – really, there has never been a gesture like it.

'What a gorgeous surprise!'

'At least until Granny opened her big fat mouth,' says Eva. 'I wish she'd just *bugger off.*'

The sentiment is not unknown to Ruby, but Eva's language causes her an almost physical pain. Naturally, Arthur orders the girl to wash her mouth out with soap, but this does not get to the root of the problem. It is simply bewildering: Eva's repudiation of the feminine graces. And this new public school hardly seems to be helping, with Eva bringing home all manner of modern reading matter. If she is not studying *Grey's Anatomy*, she is enraptured by something called *The Feminine Mystique*.

'Who knows what women can be when they are finally free to become themselves?' she asks over dinner, with a rhetorical flourish.

'No one here has the faintest idea what you're carrying on about,' says Granny. 'Wiffle-waffle, wiffle-waffle, wiffle-waffle.'

'That's right, Granny,' Eva says resonantly. 'It's the problem that has no name.'

'My advice is get your nose out of books. Stack 'em on top of your head and stop your growing.'

It is true that Eva has become alarmingly tall. Arthur insists that she is on course to become a 'statuesque beauty', though even he expresses some misgivings about her 'lack of womanly contour'. Certainly she has not yet developed along the horizontal axis as much as the vertical, and Charlie too is a little on the scrawny side, but what is Ruby expected to do? She forces each of them to drink a large glass of milk after school every day; when this has no effect, she supplants it with Tiger's Milk – a wonder drink recommended by Daisy, who claims it cured her of gout and would work for anything – comprising molasses, brewer's yeast and wheatgerm. But Charlie remains diminutive and Eva gangly, soon erupting in the most spectacular acne: proof, somehow, of her extreme nature. In a word, she has become ungainly, and Ruby is troubled by her lack of poise. She would benefit enormously from someone like Mrs Bambi Shmith, if only such a person could be found in Adelaide, but Ruby dares not make the suggestion.

When it is time for Eva to find part-time employment, she cannot be persuaded into anything as sensible as babysitting, but instead takes a job stacking boxes at the local wine shop. Then, as soon as she discovers the boys are being paid more than her, she resigns in protest.

'It's not fair,' she says, with genuine aggrievement. 'Why do they get more?'

It is as if she has asked her mother why the sun rises in the east.

'Why, darling, it's because they're boys!'

Arthur reassures Ruby that this is just a phase, but over the following months the girl only becomes more self-righteous. When Charlie helps himself to the largest slice of sponge – he is, after all, a growing boy, or so Ruby hopes – he is accused of male chauvinism. Poor Mr Yang is called upon to denounce foot-binding. And then dear old Joe – who has been their faithful fruiterer for the good part of a decade, responsible for the family's introduction to broccoli – receives a dressing-down for telling Ruby to *have a good weekend, sweetheart*.

'Why do you call her *sweetheart?*' Eva demands.

'What you want me call her, *bella?* Your mother beautiful woman. What you like me call her instead?'

Of course the girl has a ready answer. 'I heard you address the man before us as *sir*. What's wrong with that?'

Joe explodes into one of his belly laughs – *Great sense of humour, your daughter!* – but Ruby wants nothing more than to disappear into the ground.

'Had you been a ten-year-old, I would have been embarrassed,' she tells Eva, back in the car. 'Had you been thirteen, I would have been deeply ashamed. But as you are sixteen, I am utterly mortified. To throw the kindness of a good man like that back in his face!'

At home, Eva runs into her room and slams the door.

'An altercation at the greengrocers,' Ruby explains to Arthur. 'She insisted poor old Joe address me as *sir*.'

Arthur shakes his head, but seems almost to be smiling.

'Too smart by half, that girl,' Granny remarks, not for the first time. 'And getting too big. How in heaven's name will she find a husband?'

It is a concern that has occupied Ruby too of late, not that she would give Granny the gratification of agreeing with her. But to her surprise, Arthur rounds upon his mother.

'I will not have that sort of talk in this house, Mother. If the world is not big enough for our Eva, it will just have to get bigger.'

5

One of Granny's frequent opinions is that Ruby has been spoilt by the attention of others – and perhaps after all she is right. Ever since she first came to town, Ruby has taken such attention for granted, moving through it almost as a native element. Even in her late thirties, she would sense the bridge ladies performing a quick appraisal of her appearance when she arrived, and it was only to be expected that echoes should appear in their own outfits over the weeks that followed: a judiciously applied cameo, perhaps, or a rakish scarf. But at some stage this attention had started to erode, imperceptibly at first, though lately it has become harder to miss. Only last month, Ruby had been sitting on the bus on the way into bridge when a group of teenage boys came on board, grunting and bellowing in their heedless way, and one of them had actually *sat* on her. He was a great hulk of a boy, and profusely apologetic, but that wasn't the point. It was starting to feel as if she were vanishing from the world. Afterwards, she had drifted into bridge like a shade. When nobody invited her to join a table she was forced to sit with the newcomers, who wished only to speak of dog-breeding.

And it seems that just as she is fading – as her hair is thinning, and her neck turning into a magnificent ruin – Eva is finally becoming lovely. The girl seems oblivious, but Ruby notices when others notice, and privately glories in it. *She's mine. And she's going to be a doctor.* Ever since Eva started university, there has been no shortage of gentleman callers, all of whom strike Ruby as gormless: too short, which is demeaning; or excessively bearded, like that glamorous Ivor, who appeared to sport a perm. Regardless, they keep arriving in their cars and taking the girl out – goodness knows where – so that most Saturday nights, Ruby and Arthur find themselves waiting up in the lounge room, long after Charlie has finished noodling at the piano and gone to bed. It is oddly silent over these long evenings, apart from the soft aspiratory noises Arthur makes when anxious, punctuated by the announcements of the grandfather clock, which only seem more strident the later it becomes. When a car at last draws into the street outside, Ruby prays that Eva will not linger, or that at the very least Arthur will not hear. But he jerks to attention immediately and is out on the street with his torch, often as not followed by Granny Jenkins, who has clearly been lying in wait in her dressing-gown.

What in heaven's name is going on out there? the old woman hollers out, for the whole neighbourhood to hear – *Is he fiddling with your nick-nacks?* – until Eva storms inside and slams her bedroom door.

After such evenings, Arthur struggles to sleep, and Ruby frets about the toll it is taking on him, safeguarding his daughter's virtue. She reminds him that when she was Eva's age, she was regularly attending the Palais with a certain male chaperone, and nary a parental torch in sight.

'What are you suggesting, dear?'

'That we let her go a-courting in peace. How else will she find an appropriate young man?'

'Perhaps we could find one for her,' Arthur proposes, which strikes Ruby as a very poor idea indeed.

But the following Saturday, when she returns home from the greengrocer, he summons her into the bathroom. He is lying in a cloud of bubbles, looking inordinately pleased with himself, and reports upon a promising conversation at tennis. Apparently Mrs Emmet Clutterbuck, though slight of stature herself, has raised a boy of unusually large proportions – even going so far as to describe him as a *young stallion*. This strikes Ruby as somewhat untoward coming from a mother, but Arthur goes on to explain that not only is the young man of appropriate size, but – of all things – he is also studying Medicine. And so Arthur has taken it upon himself to invite him to the Med Ball, on Eva's behalf.

'Goodness,' says Ruby, foreseeing disaster.

'Spare a thought for the way the two of us became acquainted!'

He is in such a fine mood – all paternal benevolence, chortling in the bath – that she doesn't like to remind him that she had actually been set up with Eddie Pickworth. Instead, she returns to the kitchen, and immediately sets about preparing a lemon delicious pudding.

Fortunately, it turns out to be a most successful effort, with a light, airy sponge, and just the right degree of tartness to cut through a dollop of cream.

'What's the special occasion?' asks Eva, when Ruby presents it for dessert.

Arthur clears his throat. 'I know we've had a few unfortunate chapters recently.'

'What sort of chapters?' asks Charlie.

'Never you mind,' Ruby says.

'Your sister bringing down the family name,' says Granny.

'We're keen to put it behind us,' Arthur continues. 'And for you to know that your mother and I fully support you in your, shall I say, courtship activities.'

'They call it *dating* these days,' Granny pipes up. 'Heard it at the pictures.'

'In fact, when your mother was your age, she was already off the shelf, so to speak' – he gives Ruby a suggestive wink – 'so we've found what we believe is a highly appropriate chaperone to accompany you to the Medical Ball.'

'A fine, upstanding young man,' Ruby offers hopefully.

'Certainly stands up tall, by all accounts. It just so happens that Mrs Clutterbuck —'

'Never!' ejaculates Eva.

'Mrs Clutterbuck is a member of the tennis club. Coincidentally she has a son who is also studying Medicine.'

'You're not seriously suggesting that *Brendan Clutterbuck* should be my date at the Med Ball?'

Arthur recoils in astonishment; Ruby is reminded of Louis,

proffering the under-appreciated gift of a dead mouse.

'Brendan Clutterbuck has one subject of conversation only,' Eva continues. 'How amazingly *tall* he is.'

'Enough.'

'I'm not going with him.'

Arthur raises his voice. 'You most certainly are going with him. I have given Mrs Clutterbuck my word. And whatever else they might be saying about us around the neighbourhood, I will not have them saying that Arthur Jenkins is anything other than *a man of his word*.'

On the evening of the ball, Eva labours over her appearance, lining her huge, mournful eyes with kohl, and attaching a hairpiece and false eyelashes, so that even Granny remarks that she resembles a young Catherine Deneuve.

'You do look lovely when you make the effort,' Ruby agrees.

Eva just gazes back at her tragically, and Ruby feels a rush of impatience.

'For heaven's sake. You're not a virgin sacrifice. No one's asking you to marry him.'

'How terribly reasonable of you.'

'If he's so jolly bad, hand him over to one of your friends and dance with someone else.'

But then Brendan Clutterbuck arrives with his mother, and the problem is immediately clear.

'What a handsome, *tall* couple,' enthuses Mrs Clutterbuck. 'Smile at the camera, lovebirds!'

Brendan Clutterbuck grins like a labrador, clearly stupefied by his good fortune; Eva manages a coolish smile in his direction, which strikes Ruby as the epitome of grace.

After they leave, even Arthur seems remorseful.

'I suppose not all blind dates can be as successful as ours.'

'But darling,' she says, exasperated. 'We never even had a blind date. I was chaperoned that first night by Eddie Pickworth, if you recall.'

Arthur looks sceptical. 'I have no recollection of any Eddie Pickworths. All I know is that I had an Essex sedan. I was very upper class, you see.'

'And you frightened the wits out of me by talking about our future life!'

He laughs. 'Didn't take me long to make up my mind.'

'Perhaps we should allow Eva to do the same.'

She urges him to go to bed, as she cannot imagine that Eva will be late, and sure enough, the girl arrives home just before ten, citing a headache. Ruby embraces her, overcome by repentance – *From now on we will let you make up your own mind* – but Eva draws back, smelling of cigarettes. How quickly your children abandon you; how soon they become unknowable. A tear springs from her eye, and plashes onto Eva's neck. *Just the pollen, darling*, she murmurs, and dabs it away.

Later that year, when Eva becomes friends with a hippy girl, Ruby largely holds her tongue – though she does wish Tessa could be persuaded to pull the hair off her face, instead of letting it lie lank and loose around her shoulders like a horse's mane. And, for the life of her, she cannot fathom why anyone would choose to combine brown corduroy flares with a skin-tight salmon skivvy, particularly in the absence of supportive undergarments. Still, she is determined to keep her own counsel, and remarks only a couple of times that it is a good thing gravity has not yet had its way, as all will no doubt become a grimmer sight in the years ahead.

But when Eva announces that she and Tessa have decided to move out together, into some sort of student house, Ruby wishes she had been more forthright.

'For goodness sake, why?'

'Oh, you know. Independence.'

'But the pomegranate is about to blossom,' she offers, absurdly.

'I'll admire it when I visit.'

'Got herself in trouble, no doubt,' Granny mutters, with that fixated glint Ruby knows only too well – a glint that looks, for want of a better word, salacious.

'Do be quiet, Granny.'

'What sort of trouble?' asks Charlie.

'Dragging us all through the gutter.'

'What do you mean?'

'Got herself in the family way.'

'Oh, for crying out loud!' Ruby exclaims, and before she knows it she has picked up her napkin and is swatting at Granny, if she were some malevolent insect, an insect she has allowed to buzz in her ear and her mind and her house for too many years now, and that she wishes fervently would go away once and for all. 'Would you just *buzz off!*'

Granny looks at her, astounded, her face as innocent as a child's, before turning to Arthur – *You need to rein that woman in, you spoil her you do, she always felt she was too good for all of us with her high and mighty ways* – but he simply stands, takes his mother firmly by the arm, and escorts her to her quarters.

When he returns to the table, he tells Eva that of course they are all very disappointed she will be leaving, but that she can return to the house at any time, where her parents will forever welcome her with open arms. Ruby just gapes at her daughter mutely. She has nothing whatsoever to add.

The following Saturday, when Arthur is at tennis, Tessa comes around to the house with a couple of bearded young men, and they pack Eva's life into a Morris Minor. Inside, Charlie is playing scraps of Bach interspersed with jazz riffs; they sit in the air like irritants. Then Eva packs herself into the car too, and is gone.

Ruby takes refuge in the fernery. Usually she is reassured by the creaturely monkey-tails, by the cool and abundant maidenhairs, but today they seem mute and promiseless. She cannot even bring herself to water the hydrangeas.

Why do they have to leave? What point is there to a home without its children?

It is Eva's first day at school all over again.

She remembers the bitter flavour of its emptiness.

She remembers she had tried to fill it by baking a cake.

*

Later that afternoon, as Ruby drives out to Magill Road, she vows to keep her own counsel. But when she arrives, the flat is tawdry beyond her wildest dreams. There is mould on the ceiling; the skirting boards appear to have sprouted fur. Could Eva really have abandoned her home for this? With the new mahogany dining table, and the rose garden at its finest?

'I was looking for Eva,' she ventures, to a small assembly of long-haired youths sitting on milk crates.

They nod benevolently, and pass their cigarette around.

Eva emerges from the kitchen. 'Mum!' she says in surprise.

Ruby tentatively proffers her fruitcake.

'Fab!' says Eva. 'Who's hungry?'

There is a mellow chorus of approval, and before Ruby knows it, someone has hacked into her cake with a butter knife.

'Like to stay and join us?' Eva asks.

A person of indeterminate gender strums a guitar; an acrid smell burns Ruby's nose.

'No, I don't think I will, dear. I just thought I'd drop by and see if you needed some help. But clearly you're being well tended to.'

'Thanks for the cake.'

Ruby gazes up at her daughter, towering above her in a peasant blouse, here at home amongst strangers. She will not weep until she is back in the car. But then Eva steps forward and takes Ruby into her arms, pressing her into her soft chest. It seems she is wearing no supportive undergarments, and yet she is so big and strong and adult, somehow, and so certain.

Her hair spills around them both, enclosing Ruby like a tent; its fragrance is exactly the same as when she was a child.

6

Back in the days when Father was still share-farming on the Yorke Peninsula, before Daisy was born, Ruby would ride out to the fields with Mother to take him his lunch. She remembers it well: the cold meats and tomatoes, the big billy of tea, the plump cherries for dessert. The three of them sitting under the dray, enjoying the cool, with the water bag dangling above. *Lunch fit for a king*, Father would say, grinning like a jack-o'-lantern. In her memory, Mother even smiles back.

She wonders now if that was her imagination. It is so unlike Mother to smile, particularly where Father is involved. When Mother arrives at Greenhill Road with suitcase in tow, it is a great shame, of course, but no real surprise. Ruby makes her a cup of tea, settles her into Eva's vacated room, and is then faced with the problem of what to do about Father. The best thing would be to have him in the house with them, but even if Mother was more co-operative there is really nowhere to put him. She can scarcely set him up in the sunroom, perched on the side of the dining room, and he hasn't shared a bedroom with Mother for years on account of being such a restless sleeper, and would scarcely be more welcome now.

Then she remembers that Mrs Dewey, who used to help her out in the house, had sometimes taken on gentleman boarders. When she makes the request, she reassures Mrs Dewey that she needn't bother too much about hot meals, as Father enjoys cold meats. But soon she suspects the woman took her too literally, and that cold meats are all he is being fed. He is always profusely grateful to come over for Sunday lunch.

'Lunch fit for a king,' he declares.

'Shame on you all,' scolds Granny. 'Sending poor Mr Whiting to the glue factory.'

'Now, now, Mother,' says Arthur. 'Mrs Dewey's house is hardly the glue factory.'

'Yes indeed,' says Father. 'The lamb is very satisfactory.'

The whole thing would be intolerable were it not for Eva's new habit of sweeping back of a Sunday morning, as if by accident, and remaining until afternoon. But she does like to stir Arthur up with her political opinions.

'In the words of Gough Whitlam, *it's time*,' she announces.

'What, time to abdicate our moral responsibility to our allies?' he asks.

'Time to sweep away the old, and make way for the new.'

'Time for children to be seen and not heard, more like it,' says Granny.

Now that Mr Yang has married and returned to Hong Kong, and Charlie has moved out into the stables with his piano, Ruby has taken up a little job with the Bureau of Statistics, leaving the two grandmothers at home alone. She is not quite sure what they get up to without her, but cannot imagine they much seek each other out. Occasionally, she might hear them cross paths in the passage – if Granny Jenkins has taken it into her head to demand a late breakfast, perhaps, after Mother has finished the washing up. *Good morning, Mrs Jenkins. Good morning, Mrs Whiting.* As far as she can tell, the conversation never proceeds beyond this. In the afternoon, when Ruby returns home from work, Mother reports on the day's activities. *Mrs Jenkins came back from town with a pair of slippers. She quite took the scissors to them.*

It is in fact a great relief to be out and about, knocking on doors and collecting important information about the population, and Ruby soon becomes an expert on local tea consumption, preferred modes of transportation and views on space exploration. She feels she has woken from a long slumber, and is astonished by the profusion of purples and paisleys and loud oranges on the streets: it is as if Adelaide has suddenly become technicolor, and the sober tones of her youth belong to a distant, sepia past. To think she once believed that red and green should never be seen! At the hair salon, she allows Denise to persuade her towards a modern shade of auburn. At first, once it is all dried and styled, she is not entirely convinced. It certainly sets off her eyes, but she wonders if it might be a little ostentatious; the last thing she would ever wish to be is *mutton dressed as lamb*.

'Well, hello,' says Arthur when he returns home. 'And who's this racy redhead in my kitchen?'

For a time, he cannot keep his eyes – or indeed his hands – off her. And it isn't just Arthur. Even the bridge ladies are complimentary, with Norma turning up the following week flaunting a matching shade of auburn – alas, to underwhelming effect. It is as if Ruby has become visible again, in a world that has itself become more vivid.

At one Sunday lunch – with Granny Jenkins up to her usual mischief; Father grinning deafly and attempting charm; and Mother stoically chewing through her food, looking neither left nor right – Eva declares that the Army is a stranglehold of male chauvinism.

Arthur pounds the table. 'I will not have you come to my house and insult the Services.'

Eva is unapologetic. 'Actually, Dad, it was the Services that insulted me. Refusing me entry into their undergraduate scheme. Not because of my marks, mind you. Because of my vagina.'

Inevitably Charlie starts laughing; Father, sensing a joke is afoot, enthusiastically joins in.

'Why in God's name would you want to join the Army?' Ruby asks. She has aimed to keep up with her daughter, to stay abreast. But as soon as she feels she is coming close to under-standing her, the girl pulls away. She remembers the nightmares she used to have when Eva was a child, of taking her out to sea in a boat, where Eva would catapult herself out of her arms and somersault into the water, disappearing forever.

'Because the Army gives you money,' Eva says. 'And I would like to be able to afford to eat.'

'That is an absolute disgrace,' Arthur says resoundingly.

'Exactly right,' opines Granny. 'Where's your pride? Always said you ought to have done hairdressing.'

'There's plenty of food here,' Ruby notes.

'I would have expected better from the Services,' Arthur continues. 'And they have certainly not heard the end of this.'

The following Sunday, Eva arrives at the house with a young man – an Ed or Ted, or perhaps Ned – sporting shoulder-length hair and a pair of mustard-yellow bellbottoms.

'And what do you do for yourself, then?' Granny demands.

'As it happens, I do many things for myself,' he replies, in a tone that strikes Ruby as overly bold. 'But if you're enquiring about my job, I'm a vet.'

'Trying to look like an animal yourself, are you, son?' asks Arthur.

'Actually, we just wanted to listen to Jorge Bolet play the "Fantaisie Impromptu",' Eva explains, and they disappear together into the lounge room.

'Under your very own roof,' says Granny.

'For goodness sake, they're listening to Chopin,' retorts Ruby.

Distant, urgent arpeggios ripple into the kitchen, and Ruby can only assume that Eva has put the Services completely out of her mind.

But later that week, Arthur phones Ruby from work and instructs her to summon Eva to the house, as he has very important news to convey. Eva comes by after her classes, and is sitting at the kitchen bench, regaling Ruby with stories about her tutor – *He insists we call him Sir!* – when Arthur arrives, brandishing an envelope.

'You will remember, my dear, that I undertook to write to the Minister of Defence on your behalf.'

He opens the letter with a magnificent flourish.

'*Dear Mr Jenkins, I refer to your letter concerning careers for women as medical officers in the Services. All applicants undergo a selection process, which has historically favoured male students.*'

'The whole world favours male students,' Eva says bitterly. 'I was just telling Mum about my tutor —'

'Not so hasty,' he says, and delivers the *coup de grâce*. '*I am pleased to say the Army would consider an application from your daughter should she wish to become an Army medical officer.*'

'Well, I'll be a monkey's uncle,' ventures Ruby.

'Thank you,' says Eva eventually. Ruby cannot tell if she is pleased.

Arthur takes out his handkerchief and wipes his eyes. 'My dear girl. Nothing would gladden my heart more than for you to enjoy a career in the Services.'

He folds the letter with satisfaction, and carefully inserts it back into its envelope. Ruby knows exactly where he will file it: in the carved wooden box on his study desk, alongside his handful of service medals, the bundle of letters she wrote him during the war and that single lock of Dolores's hair.

*

Later that month, Eva spends a full day undergoing physical and psychological tests at the Keswick Barracks, reporting that the Army set up her own one-woman change room, composed of sheets, and that someone had been through the entire written psychological test with a biro, changing all the male pronouns to female.

'How many goals did *she* have to kick to defeat *her sister's* football team?' she says incredulously. 'Because my inferior brain would have ground to a halt if confronted by a male pronoun.'

'Sounds like good old-fashioned gallantry to me,' says Ruby.

Several days later, Eva phones with the news that she has made it through to the next round in Canberra, and that the Services will be sending a car to collect her for the airport.

'Sending a car!' says Ruby. 'Aren't you going up in the world!'

When she hangs up, Arthur is beaming.

'No better career than the Services,' he declares. Ruby cannot remember ever seeing him so pleased.

'And yet it didn't sit quite right with you, dear, did it?'

'What do you mean?'

She is not sure why she feels the need to puncture his mood. 'Well, the nature of your discharge.'

To her surprise, he downs his entire snifter of port.

'I think I was only the second man to get a medical discharge, wasn't I?'

'I can't remember that detail, dear. I don't think I ever knew it.'

'From New Guinea, anyway. Because I remember the doctor saying *you're only the second one I've seen.*'

She suddenly feels quite dizzy. 'You certainly made quick work of that drink. How about a cup of tea?'

'I won't bore you with my war reminiscences,' he says tentatively. 'I don't suppose they're of much interest.'

'What's done is done,' she agrees, and returns to the kitchen to put the kettle on.

Ruby spends the following week in bed, burning up with the flu. Various figures float in and out of her room in various states of concern. Mother is the most welcome, bearing cold presses and beef tea, along with reassurances that everybody is being adequately catered for. Ruby hates to imagine what would have happened if the running of the household had been left to Granny. Arthur has been banished to the study for his own protection, but makes frequent, fretful appearances.

Most of the time she dozes, or stares blurrily at the cornices. *There is a car coming for Eva.* She feels its presence even in her dreams, driving towards her child. It is black and capacious, and will pull up outside the tiny flat on Magill Road, where the driver, bedecked in full regalia, will step out and open the back door, and convey Eva to her glorious future – a future that promises, in ways that Ruby does not quite understand, some form of redemption for Arthur.

And then Eva herself seems to be in the room.

'Well, if it's not my medical officer,' Ruby murmurs.

'That's not happening anymore,' Eva says offhandedly.

'But darling, there's a car coming for you.'

With any luck, Ruby will have recovered enough by Tuesday to return to bridge. She knows exactly how she will let the news slip out: casually, as if by accident. *Of course, they are sending a car for my Eva.*

'Mum. Did you even hear what I said? There's going to be a wedding in the family.'

'A wedding? Whoever's getting married?'

There is rather too much laughter in the room, and Ruby registers another presence by the door, clad in mustard bell-bottoms.

'Oh, hello, Ed.'

'Ned,' he corrects her.

'*I'm* getting married,' Eva seems to say, as Ruby pushes herself up in bed.

'But darling, whoever to?'

7

When Ruby arrives to collect Father, Mrs Dewey shows her to the squalid guest room, saying he's been *no trouble, no trouble at all,* when it is clear to both of them that she has let him down badly, and herself into the bargain. Ruby is tempted to slap the woman, but instead she packs the remainder of Father's possessions into a large suitcase and hauls it back down the hallway – which she can't help but notice is impeccably maintained, without so much as a skerrick of dust on the skirting boards – and out to the car. Only after she has slammed the boot shut does she issue Mrs Dewey a frosty goodbye; a gesture Father regrettably undermines, blowing kisses from the passenger seat.

As soon as they get home, she runs Father a bubble bath and instructs him to soak for a good half an hour, while she starts the business of sorting through his clothes and laundering those items that are salvageable. She prepares a hearty Irish stew for dinner, disregarding Granny Jenkins' protests, and then sets him up in the spare bed in the sunroom, whence she doesn't hear a peep until eight o'clock the following morning. *Slept like a baby, I did. Warm and cosy as all get out.* As he sits at the bench like Lord Muck – *Nothing like a good slap-up lamb's fry for break-fast* – she gazes at his broad, good-natured face, and is struck by the way he has always lifted the mood, regardless of the environment. For a moment she wonders whether she might be able to keep him after all, as Charlie had wished to keep the white kitten that strayed onto their doorstop one Christmas Eve, but then Mother joins them in the kitchen. Although she is companionable enough this morning, Ruby recognises there is a limit to her forbearance. And so, once breakfast is over, and Ruby has pressed and folded his remaining clothes, it is time for them to be on their way. Mother issues a formal goodbye from the kitchen, graciously submitting to a peck on the cheek, while Granny Jenkins follows them out to the carport – not offering any help, mind you, but with the keen interest of a witness to an execution.

'A crying shame your wife wouldn't allow you to stay, and in your own daughter's home.'

'Yes indeed, dear lady,' he says, doffing his hat. 'And the very same to you.'

He is in fine form for the duration of the trip to North Adelaide, producing his tuneless whistle, but Ruby has such a lump in her throat she is glad there is no call for talk. Still, she keeps on driving – what else is there to do? – and soon enough they pull up at Compassionate Care. It is just as dismal as she remembers from the inspection: everything smelling of disin-fectant and unremittingly grey, apart from a lone goldfish in the pond by the entrance, as if this were all the elderly required by way of colour. When Matron shows Father to his room, Ruby senses a dimming of his spirits, but of course he has never been one to complain.

'How lovely that you have your own little flat,' Ruby observes. 'With your very own facilities and everything.'

In fact the flat is poky and smells of decay. Ruby does not wish to consider the fate of the previous inhabitant.

'And you'll be given proper food, and nicely taken care of.'

'Ain't that the case.'

'And as luck would have it, you're right next to the nurses' station. So there's always going to be someone on hand if you need them.'

He parks himself on the bed and stares at the tiny window.

'I imagine you'd be more comfortable on the armchair,' she suggests, but as she busies herself with the unpacking, he remains perched upon the bed. She tunes the wireless to 5AA, filling the room with that familiar, monotonous urgency – *Lord Ladbroke is making up ground let's see Rose of Shannon is still in the lead fancy that an unexpected late casualty in Delovely* – but even this fails to enliven him. When she has finished the unpacking and made him a cup of tea, she reminds him that dinner is at five.

'I'm sure you'll find friends and admirers in no time.'

'No doubt I'll be as happy as can be,' he says generously, gazing at her with his milky eyes. He has still not removed his hat or coat, and she hurries from the room before he can see her weeping.

Back home, over a dinner of steak and kidney pie, followed by stewed quince for dessert, she tries not to think of the slop

Father must be eating.

'How did Maxwell settle in, dear?' asks Arthur.

'Well enough. A great relief to get him away from that Mrs Dewey.'

'A great disgrace, more like it,' declares Granny Jenkins, through a mouthful of custard. 'Locking up your dear old dad.'

'I'm sure Mr Whiting's needs will be more than attended to,' Mother says definitively. It is unusual for Granny Jenkins to keep her head pulled in, but there is a look in Mother's eye that perhaps warns her off. It is not a gaze Ruby particularly wishes to meet either.

She will never forget the expression on Mother's face on that fateful day last year, when she arrived at the house with suitcase in tow. After more than fifty years of marriage, one thing was clear: enough was enough. After settling her into the spare room, Ruby drove over to the cottage in Payneham to check on Father, who was still convalescing from his brain stent, which was how Mother had come to collect the bank statement in the first place.

'Yoohoo!' she had called, letting herself in the front door. And there he was, sitting alone at the kitchen table with his head bandaged up, filling out one of his coupons.

She remembers the way his face lit up, as though he imagined she had come to collect him. But all she could think of was how hard Mother had worked her entire life. Of how the very idea of government hand-outs was anathema to her.

'How could you?' she demanded. 'How could you, and for a second time? It's downright wicked of you. It's a rotten, rotten weakness. You've been a *naughty old boy.*'

She had never previously spoken to him like this, and his entire face collapsed. Her poor, dear father. Even now, she struggles to forgive herself for her harshness.

On her next visit, Ruby is surprised to find him alone in his room, listening to the wireless; she would have expected him to have made friends by now.

'Ruby!' he says wearily. 'Apple of me eye.'

'How are you settling in?'

'No doubt I'll get used to it.'

There is a knock at the door, and a young nurse steps in. She is the plainer sort of girl, but smiles widely to see him.

'Elsie!' he exclaims. 'Best of the lot of 'em!'

'Following the nags, are we, Mr Whiting?'

'Getting ready for the Cup.'

'Got any tips for me?'

'I've got plenty to say about the Cup.'

As he twinkles at her, Ruby is reminded of the jauntiness that used to come upon him whenever Mrs McInernay dropped in to the farmhouse. At the time, it troubled her because she could tell it troubled Mother, but today she welcomes it as evidence of his former self, and returns home with a peaceful heart.

The following Sunday, when she visits, she finds Father sitting at a bridge table in the common room, holding forth to several ladies, each flaunting a different shade of lilac hair. *Oh, it was a close call, that one,* he enthuses in his husky voice. *Did I tell you about the time it was a photo finish, and everyone said I had to sell me ticket but I held fast,* and there's a great deal of immoderate laughter and even the odd smattering of applause, so that it seems for a moment to be a very jolly environment indeed, apart from the decrepitude of all present and the horrible institutional smell of stew.

He has always had this quality, her father: wherever he is, the magic follows. In her entire life, she has only ever met one other man like it – and it does her no good to think of him. *This is my Ruby, this is,* Father would say, on those Saturday mornings when she joined him on the milk boat to Murray Bridge for her piano lessons. *Apple of me eye, this one.* And the other farmers would doff their caps, or the more forward amongst them pinch her cheek. Of course, there was only suffering to be had at the end of it – with Sister Maude at the convent and her snappy deployment of a ruler, so that as Ruby ploughed anxiously through her Schubert 'Moment Musical' it felt less the evocation of a moment than the labour of an eternity – and yet as soon as she was back with Father on the boat, that eternity contracted back to a single moment, safely confined to the past, and she basked again in the distinction of being his daughter, with the empty milk tins clanging away around them.

'And how was your father today?' Mother asks over lunch, out of curiosity or duty, Ruby is not sure which. Not once has she expressed the desire to visit him.

'He seemed well enough.'

'Whole thing's completely heartless, if you ask me,' says Granny Jenkins. 'Putting him out to pasture like that, and him missing out.'

But Ruby is no longer sure that Father is missing out, despite the freshly stewed rhubarb she serves for dessert, in the Wedgwood crockery with the silver cutlery. She suspects Father might in fact prefer to be seated at a flimsy bridge table, entertaining a group of admirers, dunking Nice biscuits into his milky tea, free from reprimand.

As the months pass, Ruby is touched by the level of care Father is receiving at the home. There are always fresh flowers in his flat, and recently tiny knitted items have started appearing on his shelves: an owl in a beanie, a miniature teddy bear, a kitten with a cup of milk. *Cat that got the cream*, says Father. *That's me.* Eva is as helpful as might be hoped, regularly bringing him fruit pastilles and shouting into his ear, while Charlie drops by whenever he can for a game of cards. Although Father vexes them all with his capricious use of his hearing aid, he unfailingly knows what is going on with the horses. *Stone the crows!* he will call out, mid-conversation. *Matching him stride by stride!*

And he always perks up immeasurably when he hears Elsie's whistle at the door.

'Come on then, give us a cuddle,' he demands, lurching towards her on his frame.

The girl avoids Ruby's eye. 'Need to go on with my rounds now, Mr Whiting. Be back later to check up on you.'

Father turns to Ruby, the colour restored to his cheeks. 'Lovely girl, Elsie. Apple of me eye, that one.'

Towards Christmas, Matron summons Ruby into her office for a *quick word*. She gestures towards a box of empty Scotch bottles sitting on her desk.

'And what do you have to say about this, Mrs Jenkins?'

Ruby has nothing to say at all. Indeed, she finds herself quite lost for words. She has been giving Father a few dollars each fortnight, so he can go to the pub and make a big man of himself, but she cannot imagine where he would have found the means to invest in quite so much alcohol.

'As you would know from the contract, this is a violation of the rules.'

She starts to defend herself, but Matron holds up a hand.

'Consider this a warning. No further disciplinary action planned at this stage.'

Back in Father's apartment, Ruby is figuring out how to broach the subject when there is another whistle at the door.

'How often does she drop in to see you, Dad?' she asks after the girl has left, but he appears not to have heard.

Of course, it is a wonderful thing to see that spring back in his step, and there's nothing wrong with a little innocent flirtation. And yet Ruby remembers something else about those mornings on the river. Often, as Father loaded the milk onto the boat, a woman would step out of one of the shanty houses and just stare at them. Father would doff his hat, as he would with anyone, but there was something about the way the woman's eyes bore into Ruby's that was unsettling: some deep, unwelcome intelligence she seemed to wish to convey. And then there was Mother's wordless fury whenever another calf was found missing during head count.

The following week, Ruby invites Father to Sunday lunch with Ned and Eva, but he just smiles back at her, vacantly. His eyes are becoming opaque with cataracts, as if he is slowly leaving the room – but for where?

'Not this Sunday, dear. No call for it this Sunday.'

'But I'll be cooking a roast.'

'Irish stew here on Sunday.'

She reminds him that although he enjoys a good Irish stew, he has always preferred a roast, but again he appears not to hear her. On the way out, she checks the roster on the nurses' board and sees that Elsie's shift been moved to the weekend.

In the midst of all this, the most astonishing thing happens. Eva phones to say that she and Ned are expecting a child.

'But darling, however will you manage your studies?' Ruby asks.

'I'm sure I'll find a way,' Eva replies breezily.

Ruby has a full schedule of interviews the following morning, so she drives around early to Ned and Eva's house, dressed in her smart new work suit to fortify herself.

Eva answers the door in a kaftan. 'Mum! What a surprise.'

'All sorts of surprises lately.'

'Take it you've come to congratulate us on the news,' smirks Ned.

'Isn't it something,' Ruby replies.

'That it is. It's definitely something.'

Ruby has never cared for Ned's shifty grin. It always seems as if it might be at her own expense, though this has never appeared to trouble Eva. Fortunately, he is on his way to the clinic this morning, so she follows Eva through the lounge room – if indeed it could be called that, with its assortment of bean bags, and bookshelves teetering on bricks – and into the kitchen. Evidently, some sort of celebration has recently taken place, and the detritus has not yet been dealt with. Ruby removes her jacket and rolls up her sleeves, setting to work on the dishes.

Overnight, she has prepared a few things to say.

'As you know, dear, your father and I are very proud of all you have achieved, and of your diligence in pursuing your chosen course of study.'

'Thank you, Mum.'

'We eagerly await the time when you become established in your career, and the two of you can afford a deposit on a proper home, appropriate for the raising of a child.'

She glances pointedly around the kitchen: at the ashtray crammed with cigarette butts; at the garlic flower teetering in a beer bottle as a single tokenistic attempt at homemaking.

'We have never felt you chose an easy road, but have been glad to support you along the way, particularly given your determination and commitment. But my darling!' – and here she is forced to put the scrubbing brush down for a moment – 'How in heaven's name do you imagine you could raise a child in this environment?'

'It wasn't really planned,' concedes Eva.

For the life of her, Ruby cannot understand how her daughter – a medical student married to a veterinarian – could have made such an elementary mistake.

'Have you given any thought to family planning?'

'A bit late for that now,' Eva says with a foolish smile.

'It may be. Or it may not be.' Ruby thinks of those unfortunate girls who used to pass through Dr Fitzgerald's hands at the boarding house; she thinks of her own ill-fated efforts with brandy and a hot bath, and of her relief that Charlie turned out so very well – if short of stature. 'There are certain measures these days that were not available in my time. One of the boons of modernity.'

To her surprise, Eva starts laughing. 'For Pete's sake! I'm not interested in any "boons of modernity".'

'But what about your women's liberation?' It feels as if she has only just come around to this way of thinking, in time for Eva to perform a rapid about-face, leaving her stranded, barracking alone for her daughter's career.

'Mum, the whole point of women's liberation is that women can have it all,' Eva explains patiently. 'You're going to be a grandmother, whether you like it or not.'

Over the days ahead, Ruby reconciles herself to the idea of being a grandmother, until she begins to feel quite pleased, and even thankful for her daughter's stubbornness. She breaks the news to the family over Sunday lunch – *I always knew that girl would never make a doctor*, Granny says gleefully – and starts knitting a matinée jacket for the child, as a conciliatory gesture. Before she knows it, an entire week has passed by and she has not checked up on Father.

When she lets herself into his flat, the wireless is silent, and his pocket money lies unspent on the coffee table.

She finds him sitting slumped in his armchair.

'She's gone.'

Ruby has never previously known him to cry: even in the Depression when there was not enough money for the wheat bags; even when Mother finally abandoned him.

'Just like that. Without a word of goodbye.'

Robbed of his jauntiness, he is suddenly very old.

'What's that in your hand, Dad?'

He opens his fist to reveal a small knitted mouse, clad in a pom-pom hat and a jumper inscribed with the letter *M*.

'Did she knit it herself?'

He nods miserably. 'M for Maxwell, you see.'

'She was certainly a very accomplished young woman, and we were lucky to have her.'

'Seems she was asked to leave, but didn't feel the need to tell me.'

There is a knock at the door, and they both swivel towards it expectantly, but it is only the new nurse supplying clean towels. She is small and bustling and not in the least like Elsie.

'Come now, Mr Whiting. The sooner you stop your moping the better. You know we're all better off without her.'

She deposits the towels in the bathroom, and sweeps back

out of the room.

'In brighter news,' Ruby announces, 'Eva is going to have a baby.'

'Who's that, dear?'

'You know. My Eva. You're going to be a great-grandfather.'

'Well, then. Tell her thank you for the pastilles. I always like getting them.'

He arranges his mouth into a smile, but still looks entirely forlorn. There is a build-up of dirt on his neck, and a ridge of flakiness atop his scalp. Whatever else they might say about Elsie, she never would have allowed this to happen.

Ruby helps him into the bathroom, where she moves the shower chair to the basin, props his stiff neck on a stack of clean towels and cradles his huge domed head in her hands. It is splotched with sun damage, traced with patterns like a small planet, and has always had an absolute quality to it: gravitational centre of the known universe. But today, as she lathers his scalp, his skull beneath her fingers feels as fragile as a baby's. After she has patted his scalp dry, she fetches some baby lotion from her handbag and rubs it in until his head gleams like an egg. *Thank you, darling*, he murmurs. She cannot quite place herself in the scheme of things: all these generations around her, coming and going; loss and gain, everyone in motion. For a moment she imagines her hand passes over a fontanelle, but it is only a crater from where a skin cancer has been removed. It is a devil of a thing, old age. The way it slices bits of you off at a time; the way it removes you, in increments.

8

Ever since Charlie has left home, Ruby has enjoyed her quiet weekend mornings. Arthur has taken to lying in of a Sunday, and in the absence of an audience Granny is less likely to make one of her early-morning appearances. How she used to vex Ruby! When there was breakfast to prepare and lunches to cut, and she would waltz into the kitchen and insist everyone say good morning, affecting not to know what to do with her jolly milk bottle even though Ruby had told her countless times where to leave it for the milkman.

But this morning the kitchen is all Ruby's own, and she starts assembling the ingredients for the ginger cake. Granny will undoubtedly complain, but today is the one day of the year on which Ruby can bake any cake she wants. *Don't know what all the fuss is about*, Granny had said last night, when Ruby reminded her that the children were coming for morning tea. *After a certain age, it's shameful to make a fuss.* Never mind that Granny gets taken out to High Tea for her birthday every year, and that there have never been any complaints about that.

Of course, the best present would be a full day's respite from her mother-in-law, but Ruby gave up hoping for unexpected calamities years ago. *We all have our crosses to bear,* she has sometimes said to Daisy, but she tries not to vent too much to Arthur. Although he is aware that his mother is not Mrs Perfect, he has a great sense of duty, which is in fact one of the things Ruby most loves about him.

She has sifted together the dry ingredients for the cake, and is combining the butter with the treacle when Mother shuffles in.

'Baking a ginger cake, are you?'

'Always fancied a ginger cake.'

'That you did.' Mother plants a mournful kiss on her cheek. 'Happy birthday, dear girl.'

'Not sure I can rightly be called a girl at age fifty-five.'

Mother sighs. 'To think of it. Fifty-five years ago today.'

It does Mother no good to dwell on the past, so Ruby fetches her a pinny.

'Fancy making some pikelets?'

And no sooner has she suggested it than the milk and eggs are out of the refrigerator and whisked together in a bowl. She really is a most efficient woman.

Arthur is the next to emerge. As he enfolds her in one of his large hugs, she makes a mental note to launder his dressing-gown.

He presents her with a velvet box. 'Happy birthday, darling.'

Nestled within is a double-strand necklace, with the most elegant gold clasp she has ever seen. The pearls gleam against their velvet backdrop, lambent as moons.

'Ye gods!' she gasps.

'More gems for my Ruby.'

'You spoil me, you do. I just love them.'

'Beautiful,' Mother says gravely, as she fastens the clasp behind Ruby's neck. Arthur could not look more pleased.

'Sit yourself down, and your eggs will be ready shortly,' says Ruby. 'You're a most deserving man.'

'Where's the paper?'

'Granny's not up yet.'

'Shall I wake her, do you suppose?'

'I wouldn't do that. A lie-in will do her good. You know she never likes a fuss about anyone's birthday other than her own.'

Ruby allows herself these small thrusts and parries, once in a while. But then she feels ungenerous, particularly after such a gift.

'Poor old thing must have worn herself out yesterday, with that double bill at the pictures.'

'Scarcely a spring chicken,' he points out. 'What with a 55-year-old daughter-in-law and all.'

'Enough of that. Now just sit there and be a good boy while I make your eggs.'

He heads outside to collect the paper. She hears him hesitate for a moment outside Granny's door, but then his methodical tread continues, and he returns with the *Sunday Mail*. Installed contentedly at the bench, eating his eggs and slurping his tea, he glances up from time to time to admire Ruby. Really, it is an entirely fine morning. She can scarcely remember a better one.

'Mother still not up?' he asks, once he has finished the paper.

'I wouldn't worry, darling. Just lying in, I should think.'

Though she, too, is starting to feel unsettled: Granny has

always found a way to ruin her birthday.

After Arthur has showered and dressed, there is still no sign of the old woman, so the three of them venture down the back passage, where they hover uncertainly alongside the giant map of Great Britain.

Arthur thumps the door. 'Mother! Mother? All okay in there?'

'The children will be arriving soon,' Ruby calls out. 'I do wish you'd come out and have your breakfast.'

Arthur frowns at Ruby. 'Any chance of foul play, do you think?'

This strikes Ruby as the least likely scenario, but she offers to go outside to investigate. Arthur and Mother agree that this is the best idea; indeed, it is always good to have an idea at such a time; but as soon as Ruby pushes her way past the compost bins she sees that Granny's window is unmolested.

While they are pondering their next move, Eva arrives with Ned and Amy and a giant bunch of chrysanthemums.

'Happy birthday!' Eva begins, and is then silenced by the grim assembly in the passage.

'I wanna visit Granny Jenkins,' says Amy, identifying the problem immediately.

'How about you come and have a pikelet, dear,' Mother says, and steers the child into the kitchen.

'Someone's got to go in,' declares Ned. 'Where's the spare key?'

Ruby feels foolish to admit it, but she was never allowed to touch the spare key, except when Granny took her annual holiday to Normanville, and Ruby was able to sort through the year's accretion of junk in her apartment – dismembered slippers, old magazines, button tins – alongside missing items from her own household – a soup ladle, a pair of garters, even a single earring from the set Arthur had given her for their silver jubilee. It always astounded Ruby that a woman should have such little shame about letting another woman into her private affairs like this. And it was always painstaking work, but something of a relief once completed, as if the entire house required this annual evacuation of its nether regions for the sake of its overall digestive health. Of course Granny would never offer a word of thanks, but she always seemed pleased enough to return to an apartment that was sparkling clean. Then she would promptly reclaim the spare key. *Can't have you sneaking in on me in the night.* As if Ruby would have a mind to do so.

She should have made another spare. She realises that now. It was a serious lapse of housekeeping.

'How about I climb in the window?' suggests Ned.

'It'll give her the fright of her life to discover a man in her room,' Eva says. 'Let me do it.'

The two of them go outside, and Ruby hears a scuffle and a thud followed by a long silence. She dares not hope for anything. Eventually Eva unlocks the door.

'She looks very peaceful.'

Nobody seems quite sure of what to do. Granny always seemed as sturdy as a tank; Ruby had suspected she might outlive them all. Arthur is pacing around and blinking a lot, so she takes his arm and suggests they go in together to say goodbye.

'Exactly right and proper,' he mutters.

As they step over the threshold, Ruby feels a fleeting shame at the squalor of Granny's rooms. That this should have been allowed to go on in her very own home. Then her eyes adjust to the darkness, and she sees Granny Jenkins lying on her single bed in her white nightgown, her mouth slightly ajar. She is the palest thing in the room, and smaller than Ruby has ever seen her, almost like a child.

'Rest well, dear,' says Arthur, leaning forward to kiss her on the brow. Ruby does the same; her mother-in-law's face is dry and cool beneath her lips.

'Bit unsteady,' Arthur apologises, as he stumbles on the way out, so she helps him down the passage and into the master bedroom. When she returns to the kitchen to make him a cup of tea, she sees that Charlie has arrived, looking very natty in a bow tie.

'So, Doctor Eva, are you in a position to certify her death?' he asks.

'Not appropriate for a family member,' Eva says. 'I suppose love could cloud your judgement. I've called a locum.'

'What happens if you're standing up when you die?' Amy asks.

'You fall over,' Eva tells her matter-of-factly.

'But what happens if you bang your head?'

'Doesn't matter, because you're dead.'

'It's sad that Granny Jenkins is dead, isn't it?'

The child's words hang in the air, unanswered.

Back in the bedroom, Arthur has fallen asleep. It must have been a great shock for him, poor love. Ruby carefully places the cup and saucer on the bedside table, covers him with the blanket and pulls the door closed behind her.

'Happy birthday, Mum,' says Eva, when she rejoins the family in the kitchen.

There is uneasy laughter. No one quite dares to look at anyone else.

'Shall we make a start on that cake?' asks Ned.

It scarcely seems proper, but it is a shame to let a good ginger cake go to waste, so she brings out the dessert plates and Mother serves it up. It is a fine cake indeed: piquant and moist.

'Granny never did like a ginger cake,' she observes, though it is not entirely the right thing to say.

'How's work, Mum?' asks Charlie.

'Getting busier. Now all these women are joining the workforce I have to go out in the evenings in order to catch them at home.'

'Bloody working women,' says Eva.

'Any stories for us this week?' asks Charlie.

She did have a story she had earmarked to tell them, but she is not sure this is the time.

'Oh, go on!' says Eva.

'Well, on Tuesday I had to conduct a survey for the School of Dental Health.' She drops her voice. 'And over by the corner of Lancelot Avenue – you know, the big green Tudor place – the lady of the house launched into a detailed account of her sexual troubles.'

'Heck,' says Ned. 'Arthur know what you're up to in your spare time?'

'What are section troubles?' asks Amy.

'Never you mind,' Eva replies.

'And finally I got to the question, *Do you have any teeth in your upper jaw that are not your own, for example, any false teeth?* To which she replied …'

She cannot speak, she is so overcome by laughter.

'To which she replied …'

She pulls out her handkerchief to wipe her eyes; she cannot remember ever having laughed so much.

'What?' asks Eva, chuckling in anticipation.

'To which she replied, in high dudgeon: *That is a very intimate question, isn't it?*'

The room explodes in laughter, then falls silent as Arthur trudges in.

'Very sorry for your loss, Arthur,' says Ned.

'It's all of our loss, really,' he replies.

He is distinguished in his grief; you could almost say it becomes him. Ruby pours him a cup of tea, and serves him a slice of ginger cake.

He gazes up at her, admiringly. 'The necklace suits you. Very fetching.'

Her hand reaches for her neck, where the pearls are cool and unblemished beneath her fingers. She had completely forgotten she was wearing them. It is all too much to absorb, really. Her house is her own. Her husband is her own. She looks at him – his furrowed brow, his clear eye – and feels a love like ecstasy.

PART THREE

1

When Eva announces that she and Ned are getting a divorce, Ruby's first thought is that her daughter, yet again, has made her life harder than it needs to be.

'For God's sake, why?'

'According to Ned, we have different interests,' Eva says, with a contemptuous snort. 'And he's right. I have no interest in his secretary.'

A crackle of rage passes over Ruby's skin. That *anyone* should spurn her daughter. Ned had never been good enough. Nobody has ever been good enough.

But then this passes back into the atmosphere, and she is left with the spectre of divorce. Only last week, she had been boasting at bridge about the couple's renovations of their Walkerville home.

'I urge you to think very carefully about this,' she advises Eva. 'We've never had a divorce in the family before. Don't forget that men have their needs. Sometimes we all need to find it in our hearts to forgive.'

'I think I've forgiven enough already,' Eva says darkly.

Ruby does not wish to hear any more, though she does feel

that Eva could have done things differently. It would not have hurt her to wear a nice dress occasionally. But of course the girl could never be told.

'Just the same, I might not mention anything at bridge,' Ruby says. 'In the hope that the two of you soon come to your senses.'

Over the months that follow, it becomes clear that nobody is going to come to their senses. The house in Walkerville is sold – despite its lovely north-facing renovations – and Eva and Amy move into a townhouse in North Adelaide. Still, Ruby decides against any sort of public statement. The best approach is always a dignified silence; people will think what they think, and what they think is none of her business. Or so she tells herself.

To Ruby's surprise, Eva thrives in her new situation, growing her hair and even wearing the occasional splash of colour. When Ruby has her hip replaced, Eva invites her to come and stay, booking Arthur into respite. Of course, he does not like this one bit, calling every five minutes and demanding to come home.

'He's just missing you, Mum,' Eva says. 'He loves you.'

'I know that.'

'Just ignore the phone if it rings.'

But how could she ignore it? He'd only get himself into more of a lather, working his way through the Rolodex until Charlie or Daisy or some well-meaning acquaintance was dropping by to check up on her, and she was forced into entertaining.

Apart from these phone calls, Ruby has a lovely time staying at Eva's. She feels strangely unencumbered, never mind her limited mobility; at moments, there is even a girlish feeling of possibility. And she is not lonely, not for one minute. During the day, when Eva is at work and Amy at university, the cocker spaniels are reliable presences, pressing their woolly backs against her legs, and the evenings are loud and festive, with the neighbours forever dropping in to visit. One evening, Eva brings home a new-fangled massage wand for Ruby's sciatica. Amy picks it up and presses it to her ear, scrunching up her eyes like a dog being scratched.

'When it vibrates in your eardrum it feels like an orgasm.'

'For God's sake,' says Eva. 'What's this obsession with sex?'

'Sorry, Mum.'

'It's your grandmother you should be apologising to.'

'I'm sure Granny Ruby has her own stories,' suggests Amy.

'If she does, she's remaining very tight-lipped about them,' says Eva.

Ruby is not sure that she does have her own stories, as such. All she has are a few key moments, which would not necessarily stand up to a retelling.

There was that moment with Mr Steele, which she prefers not to think about. She supposes Arthur would have gone off to war anyway, sooner or later, but sometimes she wonders whether things might have been different.

Then, many years later, there was that moment with Ralphy

Phillips, when she had come inside to collect her sponge cake from the kitchen. It was a good sponge too, perfectly light and the cream whipped up exquisitely. Raspberries were in season, so she had arranged these on top. They were always her favourite summer fruit, ruby-red and coated in down like a baby's nape.

Of course she had noticed the way Ralphy looked at her, but she was still somewhat taken aback. Above all she was anxious to protect her cake, so when she realised what was happening she leant forward to meet his cold, purposeful mouth with her own. Arthur's kisses usually had a gentle, questioning quality, but this one finished with the smack of an exclamation mark. Afterwards, as he marched triumphantly out of the kitchen, she checked that the cake had remained unscathed. Perhaps it was relief that made her laugh so.

Eva hurtled in from the passage. 'What's so funny?'

Foolishly, she told her, and the child furrowed her small forehead and made a *tsk*.

'Don't tell Daddy,' she warned her mother.

As if Ruby ever would.

Then there were the other, less obvious moments that did not involve Ralphy, and were even less suited to anecdote. The complicity of a flirtation, like a private joke. That small room erected for the two of them amidst the group. The softening in his eyes; a reciprocal softening in herself.

The way his fingers brushed against her own when he passed her a glass of champagne. His hand on her back on the dance floor.

That private, mutual acknowledgement that if circumstances were different – well, circumstances might be different.

She had sometimes wondered what would have happened if Bill Clarkson had come to claim her. If he had arrived at the front door, taken her by the hand and guided her to his motorcycle.

It was a rogue thought and had absolutely no business with her.

If Bill Clarkson had come to the door, she would of course have offered him a cup of tea and politely declined anything further.

When they collect Arthur from respite, he has a small box of Haigh's chocolates for Ruby, and a larger one for Eva and Amy to share. Goodness knows how he procured them; by all accounts, he had driven the nurses around the bend with his complaining. There is something about the package, with its handsome bronze wrapping and tasteful bow, that irritates Ruby. A quality that hasn't quite been earned – by him or by her, she's not entirely sure.

'Silly old boy. You shouldn't have.'

She sees Eva and Amy exchange a glance.

'Such a generous gesture, Dad.'

'My very favourite chocolate, Grandpa. How did you guess?'

Eva helps Arthur into the front seat of the Vauxhall, and Ruby climbs into the back with Amy. She knows it was a mistake to let her daughter drive, and sure enough, Eva is complaining even before they reach the corner.

'How in God's name do you drive this thing, Mum?'

It has been some time since Ruby has had the Vauxhall serviced, and its suspension is not what it was. The gear changes require a certain rigour, and the steering wheel – now clothed in its fourth cover – seems to have stiffened with time, though this could equally be her arthritis. But there is a pleasure in driving it that transcends its physical attributes. It has to do with restoring a sense of Mother in her prime – not that she would expect Eva to understand this.

'It's done me nicely, thank you very much. And I plan for it to see me out.'

'For heaven's sake, Mum, it's a tank!'

'Not compared to the Chrysler, it isn't.'

Arthur chuckles, as if acknowledging his car is the same as acknowledging him. He angles his head towards her hopefully; Ruby knows she should meet his gaze but finds she cannot.

It is unnervingly quiet back at home, and for the first time in her married life she is startled by the chime of the grandfather clock. *My grandfather's clock was too large for the shelf so it stood ninety years on the floor.* It has stood in the front passage for nearly five decades, measuring out their days in quarter-hour increments, apart from the two grand tours of Europe, and that week back in the seventies when Ruby was bedridden with the flu and too sick to wind it.

The two of them settle into their familiar rhythm. Ruby still sleeps in the glorious master bedroom, with its bay window overlooking the rose bushes, but she moved Arthur into the adjacent study some time ago. Every morning, upon waking, she visits him for a cuddle. If his incontinence pads haven't quite held up, she remains on the outside of his sheets, but even so, her gown becomes pungent with urine. The smell no longer troubles her, any more than the smell of her own toileting. She rests her head against his chest, listening to the thud of his heart, inexorable as the grandfather clock. His rib cage feels less sturdy than it once did, but the heart keeps on going. *For better or for worse. In sickness and in health.*

Each morning, his bed sheets seem incrementally heavier as she removes them from the washing machine and hangs them on the line to dry.

'What's it like being married to the same person for sixty years?' Amy had asked her once.

It was one of the girl's impossible questions, and she had no real answer. But if she thinks about it, she feels towards her husband an equal measure of tenderness and exasperation, so interwoven that they have become something else entirely. Something she thinks of as patience, though she doubts her granddaughter would understand this.

The patience of waiting for him to return to the way he was before the war. The patience when she realised he would not. The patience she would feel in bed, waiting for him to culminate; the patience of waiting for the day that finally arrived, on which he no longer asked for it.

But these are all subsets of a larger, different sort of patience. *Till death do us part.*

On Thursday mornings, she drives him down to a café on the Parade for a cappuccino. The cars overtaking them look flimsy, make-believe.

'There's a fellow running late for his accident,' Arthur says, reliably.

At the café, they sit in silence and watch the life going on around them. The young waitress wears a sleeveless top that reveals the faces tattooed down her arm: Marilyn Monroe, Mae West, Vivien Leigh.

'Always good to have a gander,' remarks Arthur, as Ruby takes a serviette to his upper lip and wipes off the froth.

Back at home, she removes his shoes and holds his feet in her hands, feeling their equal weight. Those mute, swollen feet. As if he spent his days walking for miles instead of sitting in his chair, waiting.

For Ruby's birthday in April, the children surprise her with a set of car keys.

'Modernity has finally arrived at Greenhill Road,' Eva announces.

They all seem so excited that she strives to be gracious. But when did everyone stop listening to her opinion? When did she relinquish the right to a vote?

'You shouldn't have.' It sounds like good manners but she means it.

'We most certainly *should* have,' declares Eva. 'Now you can drive that old rust bucket off a cliff.'

'You know you can't talk about the Vauxhall like that,' Charlie reprimands her.

'Your brother's quite right,' says Ruby. 'The Vauxhall demands your respect.'

She still remembers Mother driving it into the carport, bedecked in her silk scarf and driving gloves. Although she could never stay long – she had to get back to the fowls – it was a bit like being visited by the Queen, and Ruby always made sure the house was immaculate on these occasions. Some years later, when Mother moved into Greenhill Road, she brought the Vauxhall with her. She lost interest in driving at that time, alongside most else, and so Ruby started taking the car out herself, just to keep it on the road. At first it was for short trips, such as picking up an extra bottle of milk or running the odd errand for Granny Jenkins, who had only become more demanding after Mother moved in. Then she started taking it out to bridge and to visit the children, and at some stage – it was not entirely clear when – the Vauxhall became her own car.

Now, the children usher her out to the carport, with Arthur hobbling along behind them on his frame. She sees that someone has shifted the Vauxhall onto the street, and that a new car has taken its place. It is round and flagrantly red, and looks less like a car than like one of those jellybeans Father would produce on the milk boat from Murray Bridge. He always made her promise not to tell Mother.

'How about that, then.'

'At least pretend to be grateful,' Charlie says, helping her into the driver's seat.

Tentatively, she backs the car out of the driveway for a test drive. It feels almost whimsical to steer; she scarcely needs to think of changing lanes before she has done so.

'You'll get used to the power steering,' Charlie reassures her. 'And never look back.'

Once the children have gone, she drives the Vauxhall to visit Daisy, who commiserates with her over her gift. For the first time, its heaviness feels like a strain, but at least it offers a proper sense of the seriousness of conveying several tonnes of metal along the road. The following morning, Ruby's rheumatism is bothering her, so she takes the new car to her appointment at the salon. After a few more errands, she scarcely gives the Vauxhall a second thought. When the children tell her they have found a buyer, interested in restoration, she feels a guilty relief that nobody will be driving it off a cliff, and then puts it out of her mind altogether.

It is not clear to her whether there was a conscious decision to relocate Sunday lunches to Eva's house, or if it was just a collective, unspoken act, a glass gliding past on a Ouija board. But it has been some time since she and Arthur last entertained, and the dust covers have remained on the sofas since Easter. Ruby now keeps the lounge room shut up, venturing in only to deposit the Vauxhall's keys in the chest of drawers, alongside her collection of fox stoles. Amy used to play with them when she was small: squealing at the foxes' unseeing eyes, their tiny, impotent paws. They look a little shabby, perhaps, but what is Ruby to do with them? Nobody is going to wear them, though you can hardly throw your disused animals in the bin.

But the kitchen is still operational, and Eva always asks her to bring along a batch of melting moments. She has just rolled the dough into balls, and is pressing each one with the tines of a fork, when she hears the front doorbell.

Drat. The passage is longer than it once was, and it is unlikely to be anyone she wishes to see. Who would visit on a Sunday, anyway? The children know to come in the back entrance.

Then she remembers. Eva had arranged for a potential buyer to come around and look at the Vauxhall. Arthur is still in the shower – not that he would answer the door anyway – so she has no choice but to hobble up to the door in her pinny, smelling of custard powder.

An old man waits on the doorstep, surely too ancient to be restoring anything.

It is only when he grins that she knows him.

'Blow me down with a feather!'

'Sweet Ruby Rose!'

He lurches towards her, planting a kiss on the side of her face.

'If it's not Bill Clarkson!'

'Remember telling me about the Vauxhall? I've come to claim her.'

'How in God's name …?'

'Saw the advertisement in the paper and called your Eva without realising it was yours. Meant to be, you see!'

'For crying out loud! Come in and have a cup of tea.'

She feels very much on the back foot, with the kitchen a mess and the biscuits half done, but she ushers him onto a stool at the bench, where he eyes the mixing bowl. It is always the very best of the doughs – rich and custardy, almost a meal in itself – and on a whim she asks if he would like to lick the bowl.

'Haven't had an offer that good since I was a tacker,' he says, laughing. 'Don't mind if I do.'

As she boils the kettle and prepares the tea leaves, she sneaks the occasional peek at him, cheerfully scraping the dough from the bowl. His hair is a flyaway white; there is a boxy hearing aid tucked behind each of his ears. Neither he nor Ruby are what they were, and yet when he grins, his former face comes into focus.

'That Arthur still going strong?' he asks.

'Well, he's certainly still going. Just performing his morning ablutions, I believe. And how's that Mavis?'

'Full-time care these last eighteen months. Dementia. But she's fighting it. Always been a trooper, that one.'

The kettle starts shrieking at the exact moment Arthur hollers for help with getting dressed.

Bill places down his spoon.

'Tell you what. How 'bout I take her out for a spin, then come back for a cuppa when everyone's good and respectable.'

Ruby fetches the keys from the lounge room, and leads him outside to the Vauxhall. There is something deft and commanding about the way he hauls off the dust cover, adjusts the mirror and throws the car into reverse. He veers around the corner in a manner that would surely make Mother turn in her grave, but when Ruby returns inside to help Arthur dress, she cannot stop smiling.

Over the years, Ruby has kept that episode in the cloakroom as a private memento, mostly hidden away. On those occasions she has taken it out, she has handled it with pleasure and care and some sadness. Sometimes it has spoken to her of transience, and made her wistful. Other times all she can see in it is her foolishness.

Why did he follow her in there? What was the message of that look?

The terrifying thing was how readily everything fell away. To all intents and purposes, that was her prime. She had a dear little baby, and her darling Eva, who had just started school, and a loving husband to boot. It was unforgiveable, really. She had all of this and yet still she wanted more. Was there no end to her greed?

If she had stepped forward rather than stepping back.

But she had not. She had stepped back. Or rather, she had pinned her hair behind her ear, which had somehow amounted to the same thing.

At any rate, no other path was available. There was only some bumpy off-road trail coursing through any number of briars, as the sorry saga of Ralphy Phillips and Isla would attest. Social condemnation; impecuniousness; the heartbreak of children.

Why then has she sometimes found herself weeping whilst pruning the roses?

As if she had missed a summons. As if she had somehow misplaced her life.

It was all nothing, really. It was just a look.

By the time Bill returns, Ruby has removed her pinny and dabbed a little perfume on her wrists. The biscuits are cooling on the rack; Arthur is in the bathroom, where he has overdone it with the aftershave again.

'Bill Clarkson is here,' she tells him.

'Who in heaven's name is that?'

'You remember Bill. We used to see him out and about with Florence and that set.'

Arthur shuffles into the kitchen, and does a good enough job of pretending.

'Jolly good to see you again, Bill.'

'And you, old boy. She's certainly seen better days. The Vauxhall, I mean. Not your lovely wife, who is as ravishing as ever.'

Arthur laughs robustly, as if the compliment is all for him.

'I'll have her cleaned up in no time. Good as new.'

'That's the spirit,' says Arthur, and glances hopefully at Ruby.

She gives a quick nod.

'Jolly good to see you again, Bill,' he says with greater

enthusiasm. 'Now if you'll excuse me, I've got business to attend to.'

'Jolly good to see you too,' says Bill, as Arthur limps out of the kitchen, but it is Ruby he is staring at. His eyes are a little rheumy behind his spectacles, and yet they retain that direct gaze.

'You know, you're still a marvellous-looking woman, Ruby.'

She has to laugh. Here she is in her house-dress with no make-up on to speak of.

'I have a confession to make. I've carried an image of you for years in my mind's eye. That's what we men do, you know. We take photographs. With our eyes.'

'Is that right?'

'It was at the Semaphore Palais.'

The Maison de Danse, she thinks.

'I don't expect you remember. But I came into the cloak-room for some reason or another.'

For what reason?

'And there you were, leaning into the mirror, powdering your nose.'

Fixing my hair.

'And I just thought.' He removes his glasses to wipe his eyes. 'I just thought you were the most beautiful thing.'

She refills his tea cup and her own, although she doesn't much feel like drinking it. But what else is there to do?

'I'm sure it's been very difficult. What with Mavis's condition and all.'

'It was love, you know.' He says this to his cup of tea as

much as to her. 'That's all there is to it. It was love.'

Yesterday morning, Arthur had tripped over in the front passage on the way out to the bathroom. The two of them had spent the best part of an hour trying to get him up on his feet. As he lay there, trying to rock himself up, in reluctant possession of that failing body, Ruby had been struck by how very young his face looked. It seemed entirely free of care, of that care he had brought back with him from the war, and for a moment he might have been that go-ahead young man again, driving her home from the Palais. *Old age is a devil of a thing*, he had said. *Better that than the alternative*, she suggested. *Couldn't vouch for that just now*, he replied from his position on the floor, and she had laughed out of a hopelessness that was almost merriment, and he had joined her with that great generous laugh, that laugh that had outlived so much else and seemed as if it might outlive him too. At that very moment Charlie just happened to drop by, to find the two of them giggling together on the passage floor. He had helped Arthur to his feet and kissed him on the lips as he always did.

The three of them together in that passage. This is what she knows as love.

Bill fishes out a handkerchief from his pocket and blows his nose.

'That's why I had to put the whole thing into reverse, you see. That's why I took that placement in Darwin. Didn't want to upset the applecart.'

Good sense had prevailed, for better or for worse, but even to say that would be a betrayal.

'Love is love,' he continues. 'With all due respect to Mavis and to Arthur.'

She reaches over and takes his hand. His skin is paper-thin, discoloured with liver spots like Rorschach blots. She squeezes it twice, and when he squeezes back, his grip is as warm and as strong as she remembers.

2

Eva and Amy are the first to arrive, clad in their Sunday best and talking too loudly.

'What a treat to see you in a nice dress,' Ruby tells her daughter.

'Why, thank you, Mum,' says Eva. 'For such a lovely back-handed compliment.'

Charlie is running late, but when he arrives he is terribly debonair in his smart suit, with his colourful socks and pocket squares. She is about to compliment him on his daintiness, but holds her tongue.

'Careful,' he says to Eva, as he fills her goblet with champagne. 'That's Waterford crystal, you know.'

'Oh, I'm the full bottle on Waterford crystal. So to speak.'

'Don't you worry,' says Ruby. 'I know exactly what you're referring to.'

'What *are* you referring to, Uncle Charlie?' asks Amy.

The girl's lipstick is a shade too dark, and drains her complexion entirely. It is a shame Eva cannot be relied upon for guidance in such matters, as any advice Ruby offers will only be taken the wrong way.

'Mum and Dad used to have us over for Sunday lunches,' explains Charlie. 'Back when your parents were newlyweds. And your father had some passionate convictions.'

'That's one way of putting it,' says Eva.

'Things would occasionally get a little heated,' Ruby agrees.

It was a shock to her when Eva and Ned were first married, and there was this extra body at the table. The tempo of it! The decibel levels! It seemed as if the next generation was pulling away from her into some louder, faster future, some brave new world of rapid-fire repartee and strong opinions. In the early days, Arthur did a good-enough job of staying abreast, but later, as his hearing deteriorated, he let the carnival move on without him. *Always good to see them come,* he would say after they had left. *But even better to see them go.*

'On this occasion your father got a little hot under the collar,' Eva remembers.

'How entirely out of character,' Charlie says, and winks at Amy.

The girl smiles graciously, but Ruby knows she is sensitive about Ned. She supposes it is important for a daughter to look up to her father, regardless of his behaviour. On the Sunday in question, Arthur had been winding the children up about the Vietnam War.

'I didn't fight the Japs for my children to surrender to the Red Peril.'

'For Christ's sake,' Ned interjected. 'What happened in New Guinea has absolutely nothing to do with the spread of communism!'

As Ned became more outraged, Arthur shot Ruby a sly smile. It was a side of his character she had not known before these lunches.

'It was sheer cowardice to pull out of Vietnam,' Arthur declared. 'Nothing more and nothing less.'

'Forgive my French, but that's *total and utter bullshit*,' roared Ned, pounding the table with his goblet.

Ruby saw the glass's stem shift slightly in his hand, fracturing like the leg of a small animal. His smile took on a fixed quality, but Arthur continued to hold forth, oblivious. Ruby knew Arthur would be troubled by the breakage, so she kept quiet, but she was interested to see what would happen next. And sure enough, by week's end there were twelve perfect crystal goblets lined up again in the dresser. It must have cost Ned a fair portion of his weekly income back then, just out of veterinary school.

'Dad did like to provoke us,' says Charlie.

Eva wistfully raises her glass. 'Here's to Dad.'

'To Dad.'

They toast the framed photograph of Arthur, propped up on the sideboard, in which he is wearing the maroon cardigan Ruby bought him last Easter, just before Florence came to stay. At the time, she had taken a long hard look at him, and realised he looked utterly drack in his worn-out brown cardigans with their threadbare elbows. She couldn't quite believe she had let it come to this. So she had driven into town and bought him some lovely new woollens, which lightened him up no end.

'He always liked sitting in that chair, looking out at those roses,' remembers Charlie.

'With one of those awful cats on his lap,' says Eva. 'Louis the what?'

'Louis IV was your father's final cat,' Ruby tells her.

'Not what you would call an accommodating animal,' Eva says.

'Even so,' says Ruby. 'She was milder than her predecessor.'

After Louis IV died, Arthur had requested a replacement cat, but it was clear by then that he was drawing to an end, and Ruby did not want to be left alone with a cat on her hands. So he just had to make do with a hot water bottle on his lap and regular refills of his cup of tea. He did pine though, poor old boy. All the same, he enjoyed looking at the roses.

'Shall we take the stuff out then?' Ruby asks.

'What stuff?' asks Amy.

'Grandpa Arthur,' says Eva.

The courtyard of the retirement home is modest, but the established rose bushes had been a great selling point, as had the Erindale address. When Ruby and Eva first came up to inspect it, they had met Mrs Windsor from next door, an extremely well-spoken woman who had once worked as an elocution coach. All of which was a recommendation, and the signs started pointing towards a move.

Arthur hadn't wanted to budge, of course. They had enjoyed fifty years in the house on Greenhill Road – almost the entire duration of their married life – and he was determined it would see him out. And in truth, it wasn't just Arthur who was reluctant. For Ruby, the idea of selling the house was a little like the idea of selling her life itself. Those layers of memories that had accrued in every room; the years of work invested in the garden; the generations of Louis buried alongside the golden elm.

But the children were adamant, and the facts could not be denied: the house was falling down around them. One morning, Eva turned up with a prospective lady buyer, Christine, who looked very sensible indeed, with her large spectacles and cropped blonde hair.

'I can't tell you how excited I am,' she enthused. 'I grew up just around the corner on Lancelot Avenue, and always thought of this as a magic garden.'

Thankfully, Christine was not a developer, but properly on the lookout for a family home. As they ambled around the house together, and Eva pointed out areas that would benefit from improvement, Christine made all the appropriate noises.

'The golden elm has wreaked havoc with the foundations.'

'But you wouldn't touch that magnificent elm,' said Christine. 'It really defines the garden.'

Ruby was pleased to hear it. She had planted the golden elm beside the fish pond at the same time as she had planted the silver birches by the front gate, and over the decades she had watched them grow. *The silver apples of the moon*, Ralphy Phillips would say when he visited, *the golden apples of the sun.* The golden elm, particularly, had flourished over fifty years. It was rigorous and incandescent, like proof of something.

'If it were me, I'd remove the sunroom and restore the side verandah overlooking the fish pond,' Eva suggested. 'And renovate the northern façade to capture more light.'

'But I wouldn't want to interfere with the fernery,' Christine said, glancing at Ruby. 'Such a rarity these days.'

Afterwards, over a cup of tea, Christine revealed that her younger brother had sat next to Charlie at Magill Primary School, and had always said he had a gift for music. And Ruby put two and two together, and realised that Christine was a Schmidt.

'It was your mother who came to look at the marquee that time! The morning after Eva's wedding!'

Christine had no memory of this, but agreed that her elder sister was indeed married in a marquee, later in 1973, and that her mother may well have come over to investigate. Ruby could scarcely believe the coincidence. When Christine left, she went to the sunroom to tell Arthur, but of course he had no recollection. He had spent the day after Eva's wedding in bed, recovering from too many mixtures and too much excitement.

Ruby hadn't wanted to bury Arthur under a rock in Centennial Park, all alone and surrounded by strangers, but she didn't know where else to put him. The only place he ever really liked being was home, but she could hardly take his ashes back to the house on Greenhill Road now.

It was the children who suggested burying him alongside the rose bushes in the courtyard. She was not entirely convinced.

Despite her best efforts, the retirement village still felt like temporary accommodation; when she moved on she would be leaving Arthur with the next batch of elderly tenants.

'No, you won't,' Eva reassured her. 'By then Dad would have turned into these roses, and you would have brought him inside and put him in a vase on the table.'

'Maybe so.'

She contemplated which of her vases would be most suitable for her husband's interment.

'And then when you die, I'll put you on *my* rose bushes, and then bring you inside with me.'

In any case, the cut roses would soon wither and die, but Ruby refrained from mentioning this.

There had been roses throughout the house on the night of Eva's wedding. Ruby had never had so many flowers on her hands, before or since. Her neighbour had turned up the day before the wedding with about fifty green hydrangeas – probably hoping for an invitation – and then Daisy had arrived with a car full of pink hydrangeas from the farm. Ruby herself had picked about three dozen gladioli from the garden and two buckets of dahlias, but above all she had been overwhelmed by the roses. There were enough for twelve urns, and five small vases besides. She filled two urns with blooms in a virginal white, with just the faintest touch of pink, and positioned them on either side of the bridal table. Daisy had spent the afternoon twining ivy and white paper around the poles in the marquee, in her exacting way, and then arranging trails of tiny green ivy and pink roses on the bridal table.

Regardless of the marriage's eventual outcome, there never was a more successful wedding, Ruby was sure of it. It was just as nice as any of the weddings on Uncle Frederick's side of the family, but in a different way and at a fraction of the cost. She often wishes she had a movie of that day, or at least of Eva and Arthur coming down the aisle. Eva looked radiant, walking so gracefully and smiling at all the guests, and Arthur was at his most distinguished. He wore hair spray instead of oil, and Ruby had enlivened his best suit with a brand-new shirt and bow tie. Although he was never less than proper, he looked like the cat that got the cream, with that great smile so close to the surface of his face, ready to break out at any moment.

More than anything, she remembers how spectacular the garden was that evening. She had spent days on her hands and knees with the shearers, neatening up the edging around the flower beds. The rosemary hedge was defined with geometric precision, and the hydrangeas were at their best: lush, exuberant watercolours. Although the gas flares did not provide much in the way of illumination, they lit the trees beautifully, so that the pomegranate just glowed alongside the marquee. Even the lawn underfoot was gorgeous and green and had never looked better. It was one of those moments when all the pieces came together. Grace, you might call it.

They had set up the marquee out the front, with a twelve-inch gap beside the dance floor through which the guests could view their home. Ruby had opened up the entire house for this purpose, and left on all the lights, and it was clear how much everyone admired it, with the light spilling out and all those flowers and her lovely new carpets. It was a house that just lent itself to such an occasion. When she looks back at it now, she sees that this was her glory: that house ablaze, and full of roses.

The following morning, she had been sitting at the kitchen bench drinking tea with Daisy, smug as a cat, reliving every moment and hoping that everybody else had been as taken with the wedding as she had been, when a man knocked on the front door. He introduced himself as Mr Kenneth Schmidt from Lancelot Avenue and asked if he might bring his wife around to see the marquee. Of course Ruby was only too happy to oblige.

Fortunately, the guests had all conducted themselves in a seemly manner, and the marquee remained very presentable indeed, with the white tablecloths only slightly soiled beneath the silver candlesticks. Mrs Schmidt remarked that she had never seen so many flowers in her life.

So when Christine revealed who she was, it was as if the whole thing had come full circle. As if she were inviting the family back into her marquee, to enjoy her roses.

After they moved to the retirement home, it was several months before Ruby returned to Greenhill Road. She had been too busy settling Arthur in, and arranging the furniture into just the right configuration. A number of items were on consignment at Sotheby's, but she had kept the best pieces, which if anything looked even more elegant in their pristine new surroundings.

'It's Greenhill Road in microcosm,' Charlie had observed, in his clever way.

It was only towards the end of the year, when bridge finished earlier than anticipated, that Ruby found herself with half an hour on her hands before Arthur would panic and start phoning everyone in the Rolodex. So as an early Christmas treat, she took a detour back towards Greenhill Road to see what sort of progress Christine had made on the house. Perhaps she would have painted the façade by now, or at the very least started on the salt damp.

When she arrived, she saw that a construction fence had been erected around the entire perimeter. It was difficult to get a clear picture, so she parked the car and made her way across the nature strip for a closer look.

She stepped back and double-checked the address.

Then she moved forward and looked over the fence again.

She felt numb. Really, she felt nothing at all.

She climbed back into the car and drove home to Arthur.

'Goodness, dear,' he said. 'You look as if you've seen a ghost.'

In a way, she had. Or perhaps she had been the ghost herself, witnessing a future without memory, without imprint.

It did not bear thinking about, otherwise it would seem like the erasure of an entire life.

She is glad the children persuaded her to bring the hydrangeas when she moved. Positioned alongside the roses, they make the courtyard feel like home.

'My God, it's heavy,' says Charlie, as he carries the urn out to the wrought-iron table. 'Feel this, Eva!'

Eva lifts it briefly, then returns it to the table without comment.

There is a sense in which Arthur's body was a type of home for Ruby: the weight of his hand, the muted thump of his chest beneath her ear. It does not do to think of such things being burned.

Charlie fetches a spade from the shed and digs a trench around the rose bushes. Then he takes a screwdriver and opens the top of the container. A small plume of grey dust rises into the air, and Amy starts coughing.

'Ready to go?' he asks.

Ruby nods, and he lifts the urn, tipping the ash evenly into the trench. It is a heap of grey dirt, a little metallic. Some sort of speech is called for, but for once the children are silent.

'He loved sitting in that chair in there,' Ruby repeats, gesturing towards the window. 'And looking out at these roses.'

'He really loved you, Mum,' says Charlie.

'I know.'

'He spent his whole life working to pay off that house,' says Eva.

'He really didn't want to buy it because he thought we couldn't afford it. But I loved it so much that he got it for me.'

It is a mercy he never found out what happened.

'Goodbye, Dad,' says Charlie. 'And may you blossom again.'

It is a strange alchemy: that a husband can turn into dirt. There is no sense to it at all. She is not crying, but something is amiss with her vision.

'Love a duck,' she says finally. 'When I think of that 21-year-old boy I met at the Palais. I can just see him before my eyes. And now look at him.'

It is clearer than this mound of ash. It is clearer than the house on Greenhill Road. Arthur's earnest face before her own, in the front bucket seat of that car he was so proud of, that Essex sedan. On their first date, she had mentioned she enjoyed gardening, and he had looked ever so pleased. *That's a turn-up for the books*, he had said, just before the car sputtered and ran out of petrol. *We'll be sure to have a lovely garden in our future home.*

3

When Ruby was a child, Bobby McInernay acquired a bicycle from somewhere and taught her how to ride it. She practised in the back paddocks, with Daisy perched on the handlebars, plucky girl that she was – somehow it never occurred to either of them that it would be more sensible for Ruby to master it alone. The most wonderful thing was when Bobby let them ride the bike to school. There was no joy like it. Ruby would donkey Daisy on the handlebars, careering down the driveway and past the ghost gums Father had planted at the edge of the paddock, and then pedal through the mallee and down towards the township, ringing the bell if a sheep strayed across their path.

The only problem was that she didn't have the strength to push off, and so she always needed Father to launch them from the front of the house. He would run alongside them for a while, his giant farmer's hand on the back of the bike, with Ruby concentrating so fiercely on the track that she never quite knew when he let go, or if indeed he had. The important thing was to keep going and on no account to stop, otherwise they would have to abandon the bicycle at the side of the trail and walk the rest of the way to school. Ruby fancied she could still feel Father there — the push of him — as she crested the final hillock and glided to a stop outside the classroom.

Often she still feels Arthur's presence in the sunroom. She catches herself talking to him as she tidies the kitchen or dusts off his collection of military histories. *Oh, you stodgy old boy.* Neither of the children had wanted the books, but they were such distinguished volumes she didn't have the heart to dispose of them. *You dear old spotty dog.* She had always faulted his heavy-handedness with the aftershave, but now she opens his empty wardrobe and inhales, just to remember. Just to feel the security it implied, the containment. Then she shuts the door quickly for fear of using it all up.

It is not that she wants him back, exactly. It is just that where there was once a presence, there is now an absence. The night after they had taken him away — after the ambulance had come and she had insisted they not revive him, *on his express orders* — she had woken with a start.

Husband removed from the premises.

That fact, in itself, was incomprehensible.

Had she ever previously slept alone in a house?

Where was she?

Who was she?

She felt a type of vertigo, at her aloneness, at the fact of her advancing years.

Eighty-one!

The asymmetry of it: tilting towards the end.

Where was the stable ground?

Then she heard Mr Windsor padding around next door, no doubt having trouble with his prostate. There was the flush of a toilet, and it restored a grammar to her environment, and she was able to sleep.

Early in September, Mrs Windsor invites her over for afternoon tea. It is her first time inside her neighbours' home, which is a mirror image of her own but done out in the modern style, with large canvases and pale leather sofas, though Mrs Windsor hardly seems the lounging type. She has wonderful posture; Ruby has to admire it. Balletic, with that long straight torso, and her hair pulled back in a simple yet elegant bun.

'And have you read any good *books* lately, Mrs Jenkins?'

Curiously, she pronounces *books* as if it rhymes with *spooks*.

'As it happens, my son Charlie brought me over a pile of reading matter. I suppose he was anxious I might be at a loose end.'

Mrs Windsor asks what Charlie does; when Ruby replies that he works for the radio, it turns out that Mrs Windsor knows his work very well indeed.

'You don't say!' She calls out to her husband. 'Wilf, you'll never guess! We're only living next door to the mother of Charlie Jenkins!'

'I'll be a monkey's uncle,' says Mr Windsor. 'Haven't we come up in the world all of a sudden.'

Mr Windsor has overgrown eyebrows that would benefit from some pruning. It is the only mark against Mrs Windsor, as far as Ruby can see: that she has let her husband go a little to seed.

'We saw Charlie present a concert last year for the Symphony,' Mrs Windsor explains. 'And we both just *took* to him.'

This doesn't much surprise Ruby. People have always taken to her Charlie.

'It's frightfully remiss of me not to have had you over earlier. Particularly now you're all on your own. You must forgive me, but I keep terribly busy, what with all of my commitments and obligations.'

In fact, Ruby had been under the impression that Mrs Windsor rarely left the house. Her car always seems to be in the carport regardless of Ruby's own comings and goings, but perhaps this is the nature of life for the childless.

'Come along then, Wilf. Offer Mrs Jenkins a scone.'

Mr Windsor lurches towards her with the tray.

'I'll leave you to your own devices now, ladies. You'll be better off without me.'

'Indeed we would,' says Mrs Windsor. 'Off you go.'

Behind her, on the dresser, stand two pewter statuettes of greyhounds which – in their sinewy form and stillness – bear a striking resemblance to their owner.

'How do you like the scones?'

Ruby is somewhat taken aback by the question. She has always considered it bad form to procure compliments.

'They're very nice indeed.'

'And of course it's a most superior jam. I drive up to the hills especially to get it.'

In fact, the jam is over-sweet and somewhat generic. The best jams were those that Mother used to make, with Ruby's own a close second, but she is not one to boast.

'I must tell you.' Mrs Windsor leans forward confidentially, regarding Ruby over the top of her glasses, which have slid to the tip of her tiny nose. 'It was a frightful relief when you moved in. I have very sensitive ears, you see. Perfect pitch, in fact. They discovered it when I was a girl. So the previous residents troubled me terribly, with people coming and going at all times of day and night. Sons and grandsons and heaven knows who else. One day, there was even a *motorcycle* driven into the crescent.'

Ruby clucks sympathetically, and Mrs Windsor abruptly changes tack.

'I haven't seen much of your daughter recently. The tall one.'

'Oh, you mean Eva. She's moved down to the beach. A lovely home, with an entire wall of glass given over to the northern light. The most commanding views of the sea.'

Ruby offers this to Mrs Windsor as some sort of achievement, but it is seized upon as an opportunity for pity.

'I'm so sorry to hear it, Mrs Jenkins. With you newly widowed and all. Even more of a reason to keep an eye on you, when I can. I'm sure we'll be wonderful friends.'

She reaches out to grasp Ruby's hand, so that their rings clang against each other. It is an awkward moment, though clearly well meant.

'I realise we haven't known each other for long enough, but I've never been one to stand on ceremony. Please do call me Phyllis.'

'And of course you must call me Ruby.'

She reclaims her hand as graciously as she can, feeling quite pleased. Phyllis is a most impressive woman indeed, and the fact that she is such an admirer of Charlie is only further commendation.

When Bill calls to say he has finished working on the Vauxhall, Ruby's first instinct is to walk into the sunroom and tell Arthur. Six months on, it is still there: the reflexive pivot, the orientation. This is the loneliness. The news – all the news, whatever it is – now stops with her.

Throughout the day, she keeps putting the kettle on, before she remembers and takes it off again. *Sukey take it off again, they've all gone away.* The endless cups of tea, stacked one upon the other for more than sixty years, have come to an end. There is some relief to the domestic burden: she no longer has to wrestle with bed linen several times a week, or even bother with dinner if she is not hungry. But the deficits are also becoming clearer. There is nobody to compliment her when she returns home from the salon. Nor does she need to hurry home, though she finds she is inclined to, regardless. There is no longer any touch in her life; her children – dear as they are – are scarcely the affectionate types. Most importantly, there is no one to whom she can report her days. When Arthur was still alive, those few things she didn't tell him – a handful of moments, really – had a dreamlike quality, as if they never quite belonged to reality. And this is the way her entire life now feels: a third act, a posthumous existence.

Frequently, she dreams of flying. All she has to do is keep her hands in motion, as if sculling in water, and she never touches the ground. The dream becomes so habitual that its promise lingers even when she is awake. It is the glancing thought – an alternative! – as she labours around the block each morning, vexed by the increasing resistance of the ground. *One could always hover. There's always that.*

She wonders now if she had felt the tremor coming on before she saw it, like something very far away. A subterranean event that had not yet made it to the body's surface. At Arthur's funeral, she had attributed it to the pressure of the day. Later, when there was no denying it, it seemed a manifestation of her dream: an opportunity, perhaps, to be airborne. Now her hand wavers constantly throughout the day, as a relaxed swimmer might remain gently in motion to stay afloat.

'You should get that seen to, Mum,' says Eva.

'I will. Quit your pestering.'

Of course she will get it seen to, but not yet. She has already had more than enough on her plate for one year.

The following week, when Bill drives the Vauxhall up the crescent and into the driveway, she can scarcely believe her eyes. She cannot remember the car ever looking so fine, even in its heyday. Its platinum grey has become opalescent, like one of those fascinating gemstones that at once reflect light and draw you in. *It's right that you should be called Ruby. Your eyes glitter like gemstones.* The car is grey, then blue, then grey, then blue, as if a piece of the sky itself had driven into the crescent.

'Coming out for a spin?' he asks.

'Don't mind if I do.'

He opens the door with a flourish, and she settles comfortably into the reupholstered interior. As they reverse, she notices a movement at the window next door, and hopes they have not disturbed Phyllis, who is a fine lady indeed but can be a little sensitive about cars arriving or leaving too loudly.

'How in heaven's name?' she asks finally.

'Elbow grease.' He grins proudly. 'Stripped her off and patched her up. And no stinting with the paint. I set up my own dust-proof room, you see, with plastic sheeting. And you've got to get the number of grits right, when you're sanding. Learned that the hard way. Trial and error.'

It is certainly diverting, being driven by Bill – quite a different experience from being driven by Arthur. She is reminded of what it was to dance with him: the animation and competence and endless chatter.

'Then I found the chrome fittings at a swap meet. Mint condition!'

As they glide down the Parade, they could be driving backwards through time, to versions of their previous selves. Bill overtakes a young mother in an oversized four-wheel-drive, and toots his horn in triumph.

'Didn't think she had that in her, did you? Molasses is the secret. Nothing beats it for cleaning out an engine. Three parts water to one part molasses, and then leaving the parts to soak for a fortnight.'

'Just like Tiger's Milk,' she says.

'What's that?'

'A wonder drink I used to make for the children to help them grow. Arthur was concerned they weren't thriving.'

He laughs uncertainly. 'And how has Arthur handled the move?'

She had climbed into the car today without much in the way of preliminaries and had assumed he already knew. Had he realised she was a widow, he may have thought twice about taking her out. People do talk, after all.

'Arthur took to the move better than might have been expected,' she says carefully. 'But he's moved on now. It's been a good six months.'

To her surprise, Bill removes a hand from the steering wheel and pats her on the knee.

'Sorry to hear it. Coming up to a year since Mavis passed on.'

At the traffic lights he turns to her and grins.

'Tell you what. Us bereaved folk should stick together, I reckon. How about you let me take you out for lunch?'

When she returns home that afternoon, she has an un-familiar sensation in her cheeks. They are aching from smiling so much. The whole thing is absurd – absurd! – but she needs to tell somebody and she can hardly mention it to Phyllis, who is out the front pruning the geranium. So she calls Eva and finds herself giggling like a schoolgirl.

'And he's asked if he can take me out again next weekend. I just said I'd need to check my dance card and then I'd let him know.'

She recognises something supplicatory in her voice, and realises she is asking for her daughter's blessing.

There is a pause, and then Eva's warm contralto.

'You did your duty for long enough, Mum. Now go out there and enjoy yourself.'

Sometimes, over the years, Ruby has gazed at certain couples and felt a pang of something. Not envy, exactly; envy spoilt the complexion, and at any rate, Arthur was an entirely admirable man. He was always able to provide, and his integrity was never under dispute. While he may have admired the female form, there was never any concern he would act improperly or bring shame upon the family in the manner of, say, Ralphy Phillips, or that disappointing Ned. All the same, Ruby would occasionally gaze at those golden couples, like Florence and Dale Robinson, and feel the faintest hint of wistfulness. It was not as if Florence was a women's libber or anything like that – far from it – but there was some sort of equality to their arrangement that had to do with their engagement with the world. There was no sense that Florence had to jolly Dale along to get him out of the house; he just went out and got on with things of his own volition. Together, they reminded her of those exquisite figure skaters Torvill and Dean, travelling alongside each other with velocity and grace. Neither pulling the other along, except by choice.

Over the weeks that follow, as Bill takes her out for drives – to lunch on the Esplanade, or to the pictures on Kensington

Road – Ruby is offered a glimpse of such a partnership. In the first week of April, they set off up the freeway to view the autumn leaves at Mount Lofty. She doesn't enquire if he used to bring Mavis up here, or how regularly. Instead, she asks him to turn on the car radio because it is a Wednesday morning and she would like to hear Charlie's program. And there is her boy, sounding awfully clever as usual. *Schubert exists in the moment. Beethoven might surprise us, but there is no real sense that he surprises himself. There's always that feeling of inexorability, of logic.*

'Jolly impressive, I'm sure,' says Bill. 'Though I don't have the faintest idea what he's talking about.'

She has the fugitive thought, *Arthur would have understood.* On the other hand, Arthur never would have handled that lane change so adroitly.

'I think it's just about enjoying the moment,' she offers.

'Couldn't agree more! It's all borrowed time.'

He places his hand on her knee, as if when something was borrowed there was less obligation to use it responsibly.

'How about we stop in Stirling and get ourselves a treat,' he suggests. 'A takeaway hot chocolate. My niece bought me one last time we were up here.'

Ruby doesn't usually drink hot chocolate, and certainly not takeaway hot chocolate, but the old rules no longer seem to apply. As they enter the crowded café, she keeps one eye on her own step and one on Bill's. Out and about in the world, she is aware of a certain fragility in them both. But he walks at a great clip, heading purposefully towards the counter.

'Hello there, lovey,' smiles the waitress, as if Bill were a schoolboy out to spend his pocket money. 'And what can I do for you today?'

'Two takeaway hot chocolates, if you please.'

'Getting ourselves a treat, are we? That's a bit special.'

He winks at Ruby. 'Of course! It's all about enjoying the moment.'

They drive further up the hill, with the polystyrene cups trembling in her hands like castanets, until Bill pulls in at the lookout.

When the children were small, Arthur would sometimes bring them up here on their Sunday drives. Granny Jenkins would claim a window seat so she could escape first in the event of an emergency; Eva and Charlie would compete to find the most beautiful tree. But Ruby sees now that there is no most beautiful tree. Together, they are an effusion of autumn colours: gold and crimson and copper and magenta, splashed across the valley below.

'Those leaves,' she says. 'They're like *coins*.'

The hot chocolate has become lukewarm, but it is still a treat. She cannot quite believe that this is all hers for the taking. That pleasure could be so readily available. That it is as simple as getting in a car and driving up to the hills, and buying a take-away hot chocolate – just like that!

Behind her is the epic undertaking of her marriage, more or less successfully accomplished. Ahead is – who knows? An appointment with her doctor. Tests. Her gradual or sudden unravelling. But at this moment she is glad to be sitting on this hill alongside this man, with that slight tic in his left eye and that ready grin. This fellow traveller – on his own parallel track for half a century – who has found his way back to her, and brought her to this.

4

Back in September, in the immediate aftermath of the afternoon tea, things had become quite warm between Ruby and Phyllis. Phyllis had clipped out a newspaper interview and placed it in Ruby's letterbox with a small handwritten note. *Thought you might be interested in this article about our Charlie.* It was an act of great thoughtfulness – Ruby had mentioned that she didn't subscribe to *The Australian* – and she had to admire Phyllis's lovely copperplate handwriting. All the same, it struck her as a little odd that Phyllis should use the phrase *our Charlie*, as if she had a claim on him that rivalled Ruby's own.

But recently, Phyllis's greetings have become a little frosty, and Ruby realises she has allowed too much time to elapse before returning the invitation, so distracted has she been with Bill. It is unforgiveable, really, and she hastens to make amends, inviting Phyllis around the following Thursday afternoon, and warning Bill to stay well away. She gives a great deal of thought to what she might bake. Only a few jars remain of her final batch of strawberry jam; although she will not be making it again, the edification of a neighbour strikes her as a worthy cause. Reciprocating with scones is out of the question, so she decides upon a sponge sandwich, which turns out very well indeed, sitting there on its Wedgwood cake stand like minor royalty. In fact, the entire apartment looks immaculate.

'Oh, you collect antiques!' Phyllis observes when she arrives. 'What do the young people call them? *Brown furniture.* It's terribly sad, the way they've depreciated in value. Of course, we've upgraded our interiors to something more modern. Wilf just required a degree of comfort, and I was far too busy with all of my commitments to care for trinkets. But I applaud anyone who takes a stand for elegance.'

She smiles, and Ruby unaccountably thinks of the pet axolotl Charlie kept when he was a boy: its slow blink as it ate a worm. But she is a fine-looking woman and must have been a great beauty in her prime. Ruby offers her a slice of cake, but she demurs, which seems somewhat against the spirit of an afternoon tea.

'Don't let me stop you from helping yourself.'

Ruby is hardly going to partake of a sponge sandwich alone, so the cake remains intact upon its stand, exuding a jilted grandeur.

'I see our Charlie is presenting another concert next month,' Phyllis says. 'At the Adelaide Town Hall.'

'Oh yes, he mentioned something about that.'

'Wilf and I were thinking it would be lovely to spend a little time with him.'

'Oh, that reminds me!'

At Sunday lunch at Eva's, Charlie had given her a copy of his new book, with a touching inscription on the title page.

She fetches it from the hall stand to show Phyllis. 'Hot off the press, as they say.'

Phyllis gasps in delight – *Really, you shouldn't have!* – and places the book in her handbag, though Ruby hadn't meant for her to keep it.

'You must be terribly proud of him.'

'Both of them, really. Neither of them chose an easy path, but both were conscientious.'

'Is your daughter musical?'

'Eva is a doctor.' After so many years, it still gratifies her to say this. 'With her own practice in the city.'

'I don't see as much of her as I once did. But then you've been otherwise occupied. With your … gentleman caller.'

'Oh, you mean Bill,' says Ruby breezily. 'We used to be part of the same set. All of us were dear friends.'

'And how does his wife feel about his frequent visits?'

'Poor Mavis has passed on.'

'I see.'

Nothing about this afternoon tea is unfolding in the manner Ruby had hoped.

'Well, I'm not one to judge. Each to their own, I say. But I will ask that your visitor park his car in the street, rather than cluttering up the driveway.'

'I hadn't realised he was taking up too much space.'

'It's not simply a matter of space. It's all this coming and going that makes Wilf jumpy.'

Ruby feels the telltale *whoosh* of the Vauxhall in the driveway before she hears it. Then, sooner than she can absorb the fact of Bill's unwelcome arrival, there is that familiar jingle at the door, as he sorts through his enormous collection of keys. It would be impolitic to reveal to Phyllis that she has given him a spare, so she hurries to the door to let him in. Alas, he is too quick for her.

'Yoohoo!'

'Gracious,' Phyllis exclaims. 'Striding in as if he owns the place.'

Bill's face lights up. 'Oh, you have company. Don't allow me to interrupt.'

'Not at all,' says Phyllis, standing up. 'We're quite finished here.'

'Allow me to introduce Mr William Clarkson,' offers Ruby, but Phyllis has already brushed past him and out through the front door, taking Charlie's new book with her.

Most mornings, Ruby hears his car draw in the driveway, grinding to a sudden stop, as if he is testing his work on the brake pads. Then the sound of his whistle as he lets himself in.

'What are we getting up to today then, dear?'

Being out and about with him is a little as she remembers being out and about with Father: that spring in his step; that ready grin, which the world largely returns – with one exception. She passes on Phyllis's request that he park in the street.

'Blow that,' he replies. 'Driveways are for *driving* into.'

She is not sure if it is just her fancy but the following morning it seems that he makes even more noise when he arrives.

'Blimey!' he says, tripping over something at the front door. 'What is it?'

'Some sort of booby trap. No, by jingo, it's a package!'

She opens the package to find Charlie's book, accompanied by a handwritten note.

Dear Mrs Jenkins, I shall no longer be requiring this. Courteously, Mrs Windsor.

'Seems I've been demoted from Ruby back to Mrs Jenkins,' Ruby observes.

Bill frowns. 'Nobody's ever hated me before. Not sure that I like it.'

It is the only blight on their happiness: that judgementalism she feels issuing from their common wall.

One afternoon, as Ruby is dusting Arthur's study, she knocks an album on his bookshelf and a photograph flutters down to the floor. When she picks it up, she recognises it from his art photography days in Melbourne, taken when she was still breast-feeding. She is wearing a diaphanous nightgown, and her head is caught in profile, as if she has just that very moment glanced out the door, but as she remembers it, she had to hold that pose for what seemed like hours, while he tried different focal points and fussed around with his lenses. He had arranged the lamps behind her so that they softly picked out her silhouette, and there is something about the combination of the sculptural lines of her face and neck, and her plump, milk-filled breasts – more voluptuous than she ever recalls them being – that makes for a striking photograph. It seemed to her, at the time, that the composition was just as good as in any of those images of Bambi Shmith, taken by her husband, the celebrated photographer. Of course, Ruby didn't pretend to have Bambi Shmith's perfect doll features, but she always had a fine profile and used it here to great effect.

She remembers that Arthur had shyly asked permission to share the image with his photography club. He was clearly proud of his magnum opus, but she also sensed that he wished to show off his wife. In truth, she felt a little titillated by the prospect of all those strange gentlemen admiring her form, commenting learnedly on camera angles and lighting. She never had the nerve to ask how it was received.

It is curious to look at it now. It beggars belief that she ever was this thing, that she ever took this form. A radical thought occurs to her: she would rather like Bill to see it.

Then she is so embarrassed by the very idea that she sticks the photograph back in the album and places it on the top shelf of the bookcase, where Bill would never think to look.

In the winter, the Windsors head up to Noosa, and the entire village feels lighter. Ruby makes an appointment to see a neurologist, who asks her to relax her arm, as he moves it up and down like a gearstick.

'Cogwheel rigidity not too bad. Feeling stiff at all, in your body?'

She describes the increasing labour of her walk around the block each morning. The way the air itself seems to have become more viscous, impeding progress.

When she receives the diagnosis, her first thought is that Arthur will be inconsolable. Then there is the immediate relief that he will never know. She suspects Bill will take it in his stride – he nursed Mavis through her Alzheimer's, after all – but on the other hand, he may want nothing further to do with her. Regardless, she will find a way to bear it.

As soon as she gets home, she calls the children. Eva seems unsurprised, but Charlie becomes teary. *I'm sorry, but you're the only mother I've got.* The following morning, Bill turns up with his suitcase.

'What's all this about, then?'

'Eva called me. You're going to need a live-in carer. Don't worry, we'll keep it proper. I'll set myself up in the spare room. But I won't be argued with.'

So this is how it happens. This is how one settles into a life of sin. Mother would be turning in her grave, as would Arthur. But neither of them are here, and those who are seem unfazed by it. The Windsors, fortunately, are still in Noosa.

At first, Bill is courteous and a little formal around the house, as if these new living arrangements require a certain decorum. In the evening, as they watch *Sixty Minutes*, she wonders what will happen at the program's conclusion.

It turns out there is no cause for concern.

'I'll be retiring now,' he says, with a gallant bow. 'Goodnight, my dear.'

So he is as good as his word, and she climbs into bed feeling mostly relief. It is a tremendous comfort to know he is there, in

her spare room. She realises she shouldn't overestimate his effi-
cacy against intruders, and yet she sleeps particularly soundly
that night. It is the first thought she has upon waking in the
morning. *There's a man back in the house.*

In early spring, the Windsors return from Queensland, but Bill
and Ruby remain so busy they barely see them. There is a lot of
wink-winking and nudge-nudging from Charlie and Eva, but
on the whole they seem happy for the two of them. Bill takes
them all out to the McLaren Vale, navigating the new express-
way with one hand atop Ruby's nylons. Charlie clears his throat
from the backseat: *Both hands on the steering wheel, young man.*
Ruby blushes but Bill laughs uproariously. If only they knew
how innocent it all was!

Back at home, Bill installs a rainwater tank in the side garden
and trusses up a row of tomato plants. His competence affects
her physically; it makes her giddy. One afternoon, he summons
her outside to show her a wheelbarrow heaped with compost,
writhing with fat and happy worms. *Worth its weight in gold!*

'What are you planning to do with that, then?'

'Thought I'd take it out the front for Mrs Windsor's geraniums. Peace offering, you might say.'

'I wouldn't do that if I were you.'

'But how else can I get her to like me?'

'Who cares if she likes you?' She says this with great conviction, as if a leave-taking from the world of opinion were
possible. 'I'd urge you to stay well away.'

Occasionally they spend an evening in Bill's old apartment in Marino, which he refers to as their 'seaside residence', but it appears that Mavis never managed to get the place well appointed, even before her illness, and it now exudes a sad air of bachelor neglect. Just before Christmas, Bill has a brief spell in hospital for his heart, but is soon released. *Ticker's still going strong. It's you that does my heart good.* It is the first Christmas that Ruby cannot write legibly in her cards, and she enlists Amy as her scribe. She dictates a cordial message to the Windsors but does not expect a card in return. Nor does it trouble her when she does not receive one.

Some nights they don't even turn on the television, but spend the entire evening in conversation, so that they both awaken hoarse in the morning, and Ruby has to prepare a honey and lemon tea. One evening Bill brings out a photo album he unearthed in the spare room, and they pore over it together on the sofa, sipping sherry. They come across a group photograph taken at the Palais, in which Arthur looks particularly fine, but she doesn't like to draw Bill's attention to it.

'Look at that Ralphy Phillips, would you? Always the dandy.'

'And there's my Mavis in her prime. Scrubbed up well, she did.'

'That she did.'

Ruby is better able to acknowledge this than she once was, with the sherry weighting her blood like mercury, and her foot resting against something she thought was the coffee table but now realises is Bill's ankle.

'Don't bother with these next ones. They're just the Melbourne years. The children and me and Arthur and so on.'

'It's you I want to look at.'

They turn to a photo of the house in Flemington, in which Eva and Charlie are arranged on the front lawn alongside Glenda's children, grinning at the camera. Once it might have pained her to look at this lost world, and at these child sprites who inhabited it. Once she might have wished herself back into it, to be that young woman again, smiling elegantly but not excessively, held together by that immaculately laundered pinny. But right now she feels no need to return to that time, sitting here alongside Bill, with the side of her leg absorbing his warmth.

When he turns to the next page, something slides out of the album and onto his lap.

'What's all this, then?'

She realises too late and grasps for it, but he has already seen it and will not let it go.

'Heavens.'

There she is, caught in that imaginary instant, glancing out a door that never existed.

But her beauty is real enough.

She feels both mortified and vindicated, and removes herself to the kitchen to make a pot of tea. When she returns, Bill is still fixated upon the photo, and does not even glance up to acknowledge her. It is such a private moment that it seems to exclude her present self, and so she sets the cup and saucer down beside him, and takes herself off to bed.

The following morning, the album is back on the shelf in the spare room. She doesn't like to ask what has become of the photograph.

Aside from Ralphy Phillips in the kitchen that time, Arthur is the only man she has ever kissed. It is as if that entire vocabulary – of intimacy – was a private language to be spoken only between the two of them, and now that he has moved on, it is a language that has become redundant. She cannot quite imagine how it would translate to another person. Nor does she think these are appropriate considerations at the age of eighty-two.

And yet something is changing between her and Bill. Some sort of idea has emerged in the house.

One morning, she surprises him in the bathroom.

'Gracious,' she says, backing out.

She has never previously seen a naked man who was not Arthur or Charlie, and Bill doesn't look at all as she might have expected. The ends of his limbs could be kiln-baked – burnished and age-spotted – but the rest of him is surprisingly youthful. *An old head on young shoulders*, she thinks, staring at that whiskery, grizzled face atop that nubile body, like some mythic beast, some variant of a faun. He beams back at her in the mirror, happy in his skin.

'Front up,' he says the following evening at bedtime. 'I don't mind a bit of a kiss and a cuddle.'

Their embrace lasts longer than might be proper, but who is timing them?

A week later, Bill's daughter comes down from Darwin to celebrate his birthday, and they all have rather too much champagne. Afterwards, she insists on paying for a taxi to send them home, bundling them into the backseat like children. Bill is unusually quiet, and when Ruby glances at him, strobed by the streetlights, she sees he is grinning at her. As the driver pulls into the crescent, he reaches over and takes her hand. It is a gesture of great certainty. Inside, he leads her to the master bedroom. There is no question in it.

5

I n Mother's final years, Ruby was no longer able to manage her care at home, and she was largely confined to a bed at Compassionate Care. Every morning, Father shuffled over from his own room to visit her. Although Mother never found it in her heart to forgive him, she was civil enough, and he spent most of his days sitting alongside her bed, ensconced in his agedness and his deafness. Occasionally, when Ruby arrived, she caught the two of them at the tail end of an afternoon walk: Mother sitting in her wheelchair, clutching a crocheted rug that spoke of her former accomplishment; Father gripping the handles, the bald dome of his head gleaming like a terrapin's shell. Sometimes Charlie came too, and she would wheel Mother into the dining hall to hear him play on that battered old upright piano. Sitting in her wheelchair, Mother remained a picture of dignity, but if he started playing the *Moments Musicaux*, the tears would leak from her eyes and flood her face.

Ruby wonders now where the music took her to. Did it take her to a place where disappointment did not exist? Was there even such a place?

*

The cruise begins well enough, with the paddle steamer just as she remembers it. She can almost feel Mother's presence beside her, as she and Bill gaze out at the ducks bobbing along the Murray: great-grand-ducklings, perhaps, of those she had admired last time she was upon this deck.

'As I recall, the boiler has a steam pressure of about a hundred and fifty pounds.'

'Aren't you just the full bottle,' says Bill.

'Goodness knows why I've carried that useless bit of information around in my head for forty-odd years.'

'Why, so that you could tell me!'

In the evening, they sip gin and tonics on the lower deck, watching the birds dip in and out of the queenly river. A white ibis swoops towards them; Bill points out the yellow marking on its tail.

'Breeding season,' he says.

'Oh, I think we're well beyond that now, dear.'

He grins. 'Knock, knock.'

'Who's there?'

'Ibis.'

'Ibis who?'

'I biss we weren't!'

She laughs, even though breeding is the last thing on her mind, and she has never much approved of knock-knock jokes in the first place.

Soon, the sky becomes iridescent with sunset; around them, the trees darken into silhouettes.

'*Ich habe genug,*' she sighs.

'What's that, dear?'

'It was a Bach cantata Arthur used to listen to sometimes, when he got home from work.'

'A clever fellow, your Arthur.'

'He knew how to count his blessings.'

The river is a sheet of gold, divided only by the dark shape of a pelican, dragging a trail through the water.

Bill takes her hand and squeezes it. 'Wouldn't be dead for quids,' he says.

Ruby remembers a Saturday, perhaps fifteen years ago, when Eva had arrived at the house in tears.

'Whatever is the matter?'

Her daughter's body had shuddered with sobs. 'I just feel so alone. If Ned's not out playing footy, he's away at some fucking conference.'

Ruby was not sure what to say to her daughter. Over the years, she had become fonder of Ned. By all accounts, he was now quite distinguished in his field.

'Ned's not the worst in the world,' she tried. 'For all his shortcomings, he's always been a good father and provider.'

'Is that the best I can hope for? Provision?'

'And it seems that when he is at home, he helps you with the housework to an extent I could never dream of.'

But Eva remained unconsoled. 'It's Betty Friedan all over again, just like I used to taunt Granny. You know, the silent question. *Is this all?'*

This had vexed Ruby. It had seemed to imply some sort of failure on her part.

'You have more than enough,' she had said sternly, as when Eva was a child and had contested her slice of cake. 'You have your beautiful house, your lovely daughter, and even a career, for heaven's sake. Count your blessings.'

Eva had seemed a bit huffy at this advice, as if she had been short-changed. But what more could Ruby have offered her daughter?

It is after she has a fall that things become trying. She slips on the staircase on the way back to the cabin, and for the remainder of the trip she is confined to bed. Bill is never less than attentive, smuggling bread rolls from the dining room, and providing regular updates on the bird life and the other guests. But the cruise does not turn out to be the relaxing escape that they had hoped for. Alarmingly, whenever she limps to the toilet, her hip makes a crunching sound, as if a pestle were grinding its very own mortar. Back in Adelaide, the orthopaedic surgeon announces that the ceramic cap from her hip replacement has fractured – *a fascinating complication* – and that there is no alternative but to repeat the operation.

Even to think of it! Just when she is out and about and enjoying life!

'I'll help you through it, dear,' says Bill.

'You most certainly will not.' The following month, they

had planned to take the Ghan up to Darwin for the reunion of his squadron. 'You'll get on that train and go to your reunion or I'll be very cross indeed.'

'Won't hear of it. Leaving you alone at your darkest hour.'

At first he is as good as his word: taking care of the shopping, and even folding up the laundry, after a fashion. The only problem is that as far as Mrs Windsor is concerned, he cannot leave well enough alone. On the one hand, he never misses an opportunity to taunt her: swooping in from the crescent as if in a drag race, boisterously tooting his horn. On the other hand, he seems to imagine that interfering with her geraniums will win him a friend.

'For God's sake,' Ruby repeats. 'Stay away from the geraniums.'

But he cannot seem to help himself, and soon enough, a letter appears on the retirement village's official letterhead, enumerating a number of complaints about Bill's behaviour, and requesting their presence at a 'mediation' session.

'"Unruly behaviour" my arse,' says Eva, when she reads it.

To Ruby's astonishment, Bill seems to be weeping. Arthur would never have been weeping.

'Nobody's ever hated me before,' he sniffs.

Ruby pivots towards her daughter. 'If only your father were here to witness Charlie's success with his book. A man of great integrity, your father. And intellect. He would have been so proud.'

'What's that, dear?' Bill blinks.

'Never you mind.'

He is a very sorry sight indeed, with the tears running down his cheeks. It is a weakness, surely, not being able to take it on the chin. Always needing to be liked.

Of course, the mediation session is a disaster. It begins with Bill describing Mrs Windsor as a *real blot on the landscape*. When asked to apologise, he throws his arms into the air – *Hello, I'm out of here* – and charges from the room. Afterwards, Eva drives Ruby home alone.

'We were so happy,' Ruby says. 'And she had to ruin it.'

'Jealous of your fun. Couldn't stand to see anyone enjoying their life.'

'I wish to heavens she'd just move out.'

'Or worse,' Eva suggests darkly. 'That holier-than-thou high-and-mighty cantankerous old *bat*.'

Later that afternoon, after Eva has left, Bill makes a sheepish return, and slumps into his favourite chair in the sunroom.

'Perhaps I oughtn't have stormed out like that.'

'Quite right you oughtn't have. Allowing that woman to take the moral high ground.'

'But to know that she's right there, and just' – he starts sniffling again – '*hating* me. I'm sorry, dear. I just can't cope with it.'

'For Pete's sake! What does it even *matter* what she or anyone else thinks? We've got our own lives to live. Can't be looking over our shoulders all the time, worrying about the neighbours!'

The words surprise her, but she will stand by them. Bill, however, does not seem convinced.

'Won't you come with me to Marino?'

How could she? Abandon the comfort of home, leaving all of her things behind. She has no interest in camping out in his bachelor flat, hostage to his weakness.

'We can still have our fun,' he pleads.

Her disappointment is so complete that she has nothing further to say to him. When he kisses her goodbye, she offers him her cheek; she chooses not go out into the carport to see him off.

Why couldn't he have been more of a man?

Ruby has always got on with the requirements of being a woman, even when Eva has scoffed at her. She has cooked and baked and cleaned and laundered and darned and sewn and knitted and gardened and kept an entire family well turned out and fed on a tight budget. She has always discharged her responsibilities with great competence and efficiency. She has never, as far as she recalls, been self-indulgent, except on the odd occasion when she may have boasted too fulsomely of Charlie's triumphs at bridge. And every day of her life she has sought to make things pleasing and presentable for those around her. She has dusted the ornaments and brought fresh flowers into the house. She has pencilled on her eyebrows, regardless of whether or not an outing was planned; she has had her hair coiffed once a week. She has maintained her side of the bargain, as her mother had maintained her own. There was never any weakness in it; she would not have allowed it in the door.

'Your father would have risen above it,' she tells Eva. 'I'm disappointed in Bill.'

But now, as if it were contagious, she senses the creeping onset of self-pity.

'How am I going to manage after the operation?'

'We'll cross that bridge when we come to it. You can come and stay with me again.'

She thinks of the weeks of recovery from her last hip replacement; the incremental gains of rehabilitation. And for what?

'Keep your pecker up,' Eva tells her. 'You've still got a lot to be thankful for. Count your blessings.'

It is true that she still has Eva, who really does go above and beyond; and Charlie when he is not travelling; and of course dear Amy, doing them all proud. And she still has her gracious home, with her elegant antiques – regardless of what the young might call them – and her three remaining hydrangeas, thriving in their pots, and her fragile maidenhair fern, lone survivor of the fernery.

But the flat feels emptier for having been emptied a second time. The grinding sound in her hip has become unbearable – a jeering assertion of decrepitude – so she spends much of her day in bed. Her tremor is now so insistent that she drops her eyebrow pencil, fracturing it on the bathroom tiles; the stiffness spreads from her hip up through her back, so she can no longer lift her arms to wash her hair. When she trips in the sunroom, she experiences it as a type of assault. There is a rush of heat to her smitten nose; tears spring from her eyes. As she patches herself up in the bathroom, she feels a morbid curiosity at the spectre in the mirror: that lank hair; that angry nose; that featureless, unmade-up face. Never before has she let herself go to seed. But what does it matter? There is no longer anyone to look.

The doorbell startles her with a flare of hope. But it is only Mrs Windsor, proffering a tray of jam tartlets like a Girl Guide.

'I remembered how much you admired my strawberry jam, so Wilf drove me up to the hills to get some more.'

If only Eva were here to slam the door in her face; Ruby cannot quite bring herself to do it. Instead, she accepts the tartlets with a curt thank you, and conveys them to the kitchen. Much as it goes against the grain to waste good food, she tips them into a kitchen tidy bag, where they concuss gently against each other and then crumble: clearly, Mrs Windsor makes a tender crust. Then she seals the bag, puts it in the garbage bin and takes herself off to bed.

The following morning, she has only just put the kettle on when Eva arrives.

'What are you doing here so early?'

Eva looks concerned. 'Mum, it's six o'clock at night. I was on my way home from work and thought I'd check up on you.'

Ruby feels a mild vertigo; the morning darkness changes complexion and becomes evening.

'Are you taking proper care of yourself?'

'Don't you worry about me.'

'How's that Bill?'

'I wouldn't know.'

She has not heard from him, and is determined not to call him herself. At the same time, she is forever conscious of the silent telephone. Each time it rings, her heart starts pounding – but it is always just Eva checking up on her, or Daisy relating the latest goings-on within the homeopathy society.

'I can only assume he's on the Ghan by now, headed up to Darwin to see all his old boys.'

'Perhaps you might find it in your heart to forgive him.'

She snorts. 'I'm certainly not asking him back.'

The problem is that she misses him. That's the rub. She misses his jaunty walk, his constant stream of conversation. She misses the twinkle in his eye, the way it illuminates all the possibility in a room. She misses the delinquent feeling of being out and about with him, the truancy it offered from old age. He was deteriorating, and hard of hearing, and weaker than she had allowed herself to believe. And yet he led her towards life rather than away from it.

The morning of the operation, Eva helps Ruby into the bathroom, where she drapes a towel over her shoulders and guides her neck back over the lip of the basin.

'Is that comfortable enough?'

It is in fact terribly uncomfortable, but nonetheless there is some great physical truth in having her hair lathered up by her daughter's strong, competent fingers.

'It's *lover-ly,*' she murmurs. 'Always loved a good shampoo.'

When she was a child, Sunday night had been hair-washing night at the farm. Mother approached the task with the same grim efficiency she brought to any household chore, as if determined there would be no pleasure found in it. There was always a good deal of scrubbing and yanking, and large quantities of soap in the eye, alongside stern admonitions not to cry, and yet for Ruby, the net effect of those Sunday evenings, which began with warm water heaved in from the stove and concluded with Mother sitting at the piano, was of an almost wanton ravishment and access to beauty.

After their bath, the girls were allowed to remain up by the stove to dry their hair. Father would sit at the table, filling out a coupon, while Mother would finish the drying and scrubbing and sweeping and folding before finally, should the mood take her, sitting down at the piano to play. An astonishing lightness issued from the piano – an entwined joy and melancholy. There was no moment in the week to match it: the warmth of the stove against the back of Ruby's neck; the sound filling the house. Once, she had heard Mrs McInernay tell little Lottie that she loved her, which struck her as an astonishing thing to say to a daughter. On such Sunday nights it was clear that these things never needed to be said. It was enough to know them.

'Don't cry, Mum,' says Eva, as she rinses. 'We'll get you through this.'

'It's just the shampoo, dear. It irritates my eyes.'

She must stop thinking about her parents. It undoes her: all this scalp interference, this immersion in the past.

When Eva has dried her hair, it is too big and blowsy, but at least the face in the mirror is a recognisable version of her own, rather than that crone who had been peering out at her over recent days.

'You don't look happy, Mum. What's the matter?'

'I miss my eyebrows,' Ruby confesses. 'Don't want to die without my eyebrows.'

'No one's going to die,' says Eva. 'At least not without my permission.'

But on the way to the hospital, she stops at a pharmacy, and returns to the car with a make-up pencil. She leans towards Ruby in the passenger street, and painstakingly draws on her brows.

'Not too thick, darling. And don't forget to feather them a little.'

'Don't worry. I think I know what you look like by now.'

As she draws, Eva holds her breath and releases it in small puffs, as she did when she was a child, doing her colouring-in.

'On the subject of Ned,' Ruby offers. 'You're better off without him.'

'What do you mean?'

Ruby glances out at the gaudy sign, *Midnight Pharmacy*, with its purple letters set against an orange circle.

'Just that I love you and I'm proud of you,' she says hurriedly.

Eva stops drawing for a moment, leans in and kisses her.

'Thank you, Mum. And I love you.'

At the hospital, Eva leaves her in the waiting room, promising to return after work.

'Remember, there's to be no dying. Even with such fine-looking eyebrows.'

And then Ruby is on a bed, being wheeled into theatre. She recognises the anaesthetist from last time, that same pale stare behind his mask. He holds the tube over her mouth. *Go to sleep now.* It may be the last thing she ever hears, which does not especially perturb her.

Ich habe genug.

But she emerges soon enough and finds Father in the room. He is piled up with gifts for her: chocolates and pastilles and the most beautiful set of jade beads.

A photo finish it was. The last race, and everybody at Victoria Park wanted to buy that ticket from me, even the bookmakers. But I stuck to my guns, I did. Made a killing.

She closes her eyes, knowing Mother will confiscate the beads; they are lovely, but not suitable for a child.

When she opens her eyes for a second time, it is not Father but Bill. His hands are empty. There are no beads, but it is a great comfort to see him.

Will you forgive me?

Of course, she says, or thinks she says. He climbs into bed with her, so that she can feel his body warm against her own. The faintest light creeps through the venetian blinds, and it takes her a moment to get her bearings. Then she realises they are back in the retirement home on their first night together in bed. She remembers every moment, as she knew she would at the time, for as long as she would live. Next door, a chair is scraped across the floor, and a television abruptly switched off. Then the outside world falls away completely. There is no longer any audience; it is only the two of them.

She is not sure what Bill sees when he looks at her, what form she takes. Nor is she entirely sure who she sees, who is this silhouette in her bed. He wraps his arms around her and kisses her, and she is a girl again, but also an octogenarian woman with her octogenarian love, his bristly whiskers pressed against her upper lip.

What's it like then, being kissed by an old man?

She is surprised by the girlishness of her laughter. *Not so different from being kissed by a young man.*

His lips are soft, but when she rests her forehead against his, she senses the bony proximity of their skulls and feels a compassion for them both – and for Arthur and Mavis too, whose imprints remain in the way they touch each other – and an astonishment at how far they have moved through time. She reaches downward, but he takes her hand in his own and gently moves it away. *Might we just embrace?* So she turns and he spoons her, crossing his arms around her chest and taking a breast in each of his hands. She feels her body change beneath his touch. Its tremor is stilled. Its melancholy gives way to something else. How glad he makes her. As if an ending could also be a beginning. As if a former body could be returned to her. Not the body of that woman in the photograph, but an earlier, more fundamental body. The first known body. The still and steady thing.

Acknowledgements

I would like to thank the storytelling women of my family for decades of anecdote, wit and embellishment: Helen Goldsworthy, Virginia Beagley, Janet Sherban and the late Molly Wharldall. Thank you to my long-term collaborator Chris Feik at Black Inc.; to Jo Rosenberg and Kirstie Innes-Will, also at Black Inc., for their delicate editorial touches; and to my friend and agent Clare Forster. I am indebted to Jade Maitre, Peter Goldsworthy, Nicholas Purcell and particularly Chloe Hooper for their close, forensic reads. Donata Carrazza, Michael Shmith, Helen Ayres, Richard Wharldall, Mary Maitland, Jennifer Rutherford, Andrew Haveron, Melanie Stephenson, Nick Mathew, Sophie Dunstone, Tom Robinson, Daniel Goldsworthy, Alex Goldsworthy and Reuben and Otto Purcell generously provided clarifications and suggestions. Excerpts of the text have previously appeared in *The Monthly* and *Griffith Review*. I am grateful to the Ukaria Cultural Centre, the J.M. Coetzee Centre for Creative Practice, *Griffith Review*, Varuna, Janet Clarke Hall, Arts SA and the Australia Council for residencies and support.

Anna Goldsworthy is the author of *Piano Lessons*, *Welcome to Your New Life* and the Quarterly Essay *Unfinished Business: Sex, Freedom and Misogyny*. Her writing has appeared in *The Monthly*, *The Age*, *The Australian*, the *Adelaide Review* and *The Best Australian Essays*. She is also a concert pianist, with several recordings to her name, and a lecturer at the Elder Conservatorium of Music.

CPSIA information can be obtained
at www.ICGtesting.com
Printed in the USA
BVHW032249260123
657282BV00018B/144